Stories to Share with My Partner
Book 5

A Northport Booksellers Publication

José F. Nodar

Stories to Share with My Partner Book 5 / José F. Nodar
ISBN: 978-0-9756618-2-6 - Paperback
ISBN: 978-0-9756618-3-3 - e-Book
ISBN: 978-0-9756618-4-0 - Audiobook

Dedication

First and foremost, to my wife Miriam, who is always my muse, my inspiration, and has made everything wonderful in my life.

Also, to my daughter Anna, and my stepdaughters Elizabeth and Allison, who give encouragement and their love.

To my grandchildren Rachel and David and my step granddaughter Andrea, who have contributed to my life without them even knowing it.

To my friends of many years and most recent ones who have tolerated me discussing my ideas ad nauseam.

To the talented artists who have helped make me look good on these pages through their copyediting and proofreading, book cover design, and narration of the audiobook. I am in your debt.

Finally, to my fellow authors, and those who have supported me through my journey as an author. I appreciate you.

Table of Contents

We Got Ourselves a New Car 4

A Celestial Sweep 21

You 25

Best Friends 27

Lesson # 23 – How to Support Your Wife 38

Lemons 44

Killing My Darling 53

Special Holiday 61

What A Worthless Guarantee 65

The Invention of Dating 77

When True Love Arrives 80

We Are Going to Write 87

Change 94

What's For Dinner 99

Marriage is in the Cards 106

Until Death Do Us Apart 113

Accolades 128

Spanked 133

Unpredictable Skies 144

The E-Phone 26 Conspiracy 151

You Can't Always Get What You Want 158

Making Millions..162

One Rotten Apple Spoils The Barrel 171

Whispers Of the Past..175

The Best Christmas Present..187

3

Share Market 192
About the Author 196

We Got Ourselves a New Car

Jeremy and Susan exchanged puzzled looks as they peered out of their bedroom window on Sunday morning. There, in their driveway, sat an abandoned car, still running and with its key still inside. With the bright morning sun glinting off the car's sleek exterior, it was impossible to miss.

Jeremy, a tall man with a penchant for adventure, was the first to speak up.

"Susan, are you seeing this? Whose car is that, and how did it end up in our driveway?"

Susan, a bit more cautious and concerned about the unexpected situation, replied, "I don't know, Jeremy. It certainly wasn't here last night. Maybe we should call the police and report it?"

Jeremy scratched his head, contemplating the situation.

"Before we involve the police, let's take a closer look. Maybe there's a clue inside that can help us figure out whose car it is and why it's here."

Together, they walked down the stairs, crossed the living room, and stepped outside onto their front porch. The car, a black sedan, seemed to be in good condition. Jeremy cautiously approached the driver's side while Susan stood nearby, her eyes scanning their surroundings for any signs of unusual activity.

Jeremy opened the car door carefully and peered inside. The interior appeared tidy, with no obvious signs of struggle or distress. The key was in the ignition. He spotted a small envelope lying on the passenger seat. When he picked it up, he saw that the words *For Jeremy and Susan* were written on the front in elegant script.

With a mixture of curiosity and apprehension, Jeremy opened the envelope and found a handwritten note inside. It read: *Dear Jeremy and Susan. We apologize for the intrusion, but we had no other option. We'll explain everything soon. Please take care of the car for us. We promise to return for it in a few days. Sincerely, A Friend.*

Jeremy read the letter aloud so Susan could hear. Once Jeremy finished reading the letter aloud, he and Susan exchanged bewildered glances, trying to decipher the meaning of the mysterious note. Who were these people, and what had driven them to leave their car in their driveway? The note offered more questions than answers.

After some deliberation, they turned off the ignition, took the key and left the car in their driveway for the time being, hoping that the mysterious friend would indeed return for it as promised. Jeremy and Susan spent the rest of the morning and much of the afternoon discussing various scenarios and trying to make sense of the unusual situation, eager to uncover the mystery that had unexpectedly landed on their doorstep.

In the middle of their discussion, the blaring of a car horn startled the couple. Jeremy and Susan exchanged alarmed glances before rushing back outside to investigate the source of the noise. Opening the front door, they noticed that the black sedan's headlights were flashing in sync with the horn's beeps.

Jeremy quickly retrieved the key and opened the front door, thinking that someone was trying to steal the vehicle. However, to his surprise, the car was empty. He stared at the driver's seat, key in hand, absolutely confounded. There was no sign that anyone or anything had been honking the horn.

Susan, seeing that there was no danger, came up beside him and asked, "Jeremy, what's going on? Why would the car suddenly start honking like this?"

Jeremy, equally puzzled, replied, "I have no idea. It's as if the car has a mind of its own."

The two of them stood there and stared at the vehicle, waiting for something to happen. Sure enough, the car's horn and flashing headlights started back up. They insert the key into the ignition and turned the engine off, but the car's electrical systems seemed to malfunction. The horn blared on, and the headlights continued to flash.

The din was attracting neighbours, who gathered around their house and stared at the car. Their expressions ranged from bewildered to annoyed. One asked: "Susan, is this your new car? It's going crazy."

"No, it's not. We've been looking for one, but this isn't it. We just found it here this morning."

Someone suggested calling the local towing company to move the car from their driveway. Thinking that was an excellent idea, Susan made the call. A tow truck was dispatched, and in less than ten minutes, it arrived to find the horn still honking and the lights still shining. Jeremy and Susan explained the strange circumstances to the driver, who was quite startled by their story.

The tow truck driver carefully manoeuvred his equipment to hook up the car for towing. As he did so, the horn and flashing lights finally ceased. Jeremy and Susan watched with a mixture of relief and confusion as their mysterious guest was about to be towed away.

Just as the car was being lifted onto the tow truck, a small piece of paper fluttered out from under the driver's seat. Jeremy picked it off the ground and saw that it was another note. This one read: *Apologies for the unexpected commotion. Please keep it safe for us a little while longer. We'll be in touch soon. Sincerely, Your Persistent Friend.*

Jeremy and Susan exchanged incredulous looks. This situation had taken another unexpected turn, leaving them with even more questions than before. However, it was clear that this 'persistent friend' either expected the noise and lights or had somehow slipped another note in while they weren't looking. That they were being watched disturbed Jeremy and

Susan, who kept the car after all, especially now that the lights were off, and the horn wasn't honking incessantly. However, they didn't want it in the driveway. Instead, they arranged for it to be parked on the street in front of their house.

The tow truck driver complied and dropped off the car on the street as requested. Then he came up and handed Jeremy the bill: $199.00!

"You must be joking."

"No sir. This is the total of the call out fee, hook up fee and drop off fee. All standard. For payment, you can use EFTPOS or B-Pay. Thank you for using ACME Towing Service," the driver said with a genial smile. With that, he drove off, leaving Jeremy and Susan standing on their footpath.

They watched the driver leave. They were peeved at the bill, but it was nothing they couldn't handle financially. The important thing was that the car wasn't in their driveway, nor was it disturbing them and the neighbours. The couple walked back to their house, when suddenly, the light and racket started again. This time the horn was louder, and it gradually increased in volume to where Susan had to cover her ears, afraid they might burst.

"I've had it with this piece of junk!" Jeremy roared. He went to his shed in the backyard and brought out a sledgehammer, which he promptly took to the vehicle.

Jeremy started on the bonnet and worked his way around the driver's side of the car, but the horn and lights continued to sound out and flash. As he futilely laid into the car, an idea occurred to Susan, who shouted: "Jeremy, bust out all the headlights and rear lights!"

Jeremy complied, smashing them in before starting on the roof of the car. He hammered down on it with such force that he made a hole in the top, allowing him to see the interior. But his rampage wasn't done yet; he then worked along the passenger side, thoroughly wrecking the black sedan.

After 20 minutes, the car was reduced to little more than tyres and a heap of scrap metal. The neighbours, who had once again come out to see what was going on, clapped Jeremy on the back for destroying the obnoxious vehicle. Satisfied that there would be no more noise, they all went back to their houses after congratulating and thanking the couple. Susan escorted a tired-out Jeremy back to the house as he dragged his sledgehammer along the road behind him. His arms ached, and he wanted nothing more than to lie down.

Then they heard another horn.

Jeremy and Susan, fearful that the black sedan somehow had some life left in it, turned around to see two brand-new sedans, one white and one back, pulling up on their driveway. Two men in black suits with white shirts and black ties got out of the car and walked up to them.

"Jeremy, Susan, we have instructions from your friend to leave the white sedan here. Here is the key. Have a lovely day."

Before Susan or Jeremy could say anything, the men got in the black car and left.

"Jeremy, what the hell is going on? Who were those men?"

"I'm as surprised as you are, Susan. But if that white sedan's anything like the other one, I'll lose my mind," Jeremy replied, hefting his sledgehammer as best he could with his tired arms.

Susan cautiously approached the white sedan, the key in her hand. She turned to Jeremy; her expression filled with uncertainty. She was terrified to touch it, lest she set off the horn and lights.

"Do you think I should open it?"

Jeremy was equally nervous, but tried to stay composed.

"I don't think so. I mean, we don't even know who those men were, let alone this 'friend' who keeps leaving these damn cars." Susan let out a sigh of relief, happy to have Jeremy's agreement.

"Yes, you're right. Let's get inside, lock the doors, and call all of our friends to see who's sending us these cars. We need to find out what's going on."

Jeremy and Susan spent an hour calling their friends. None of them had any idea what they were talking about; most assumed it was just a prank. Periodically, they looked out the window at the white sedan on the street. It made no sound, and the lights stayed off, and yet somehow it was even more unsettling than the black sedan before it.

The couple was almost done making calls. They just had one more friend to ask: Peter. He picked up after a few rings.

"Hello?"

"Hey, it's Jeremy. We're calling about the guys that just dropped off a white sedan for us. Do you know anything about this?"

There was a pause on the other end of the line. Jeremy put the call on speakerphone, and when Peter responded, his voice sounded tense.

"Jeremy, listen carefully. I can't explain everything over the phone, but you need to take that car and drive to the address I'm going to text you. It's crucial that you do this now, and I promise I'll explain everything when you get there. Trust me, it's for your own safety."

Jeremy exchanged another glance with Susan, whose eyes were wide and darting around the room, as if she feared the car might somehow get inside.

"OK, we'll do it, but you better have some answers when we arrive," Jeremy replied before hanging up. Then he went upstairs and opened his gun safe. He took out his Smith & Wesson Model 686. This revolver was chambered for the powerful .357 Magnum cartridge, known for its stopping power. It typically had a 6 or 7-round cylinder capacity and was a favourite among law enforcement. Jeremy could easily carry it under his coat. One of the main reasons he bought the gun was for self-defence. He hoped he'd never have to use it that way, but there was no telling what awaited him where Peter was asking him to go. He loaded the gun and walked downstairs to show Susan, who was wringing her hands and staring out the window.

"Do you think we'll need it?"

"I'm not sure where we're going, but I'm not taking any chances. Are you OK if I bring it?"

"Yes sweetie," was all Susan said.

When they left, the sun was setting. They were reluctant to get in the white sedan, but eventually they did. Jeremy was in the driver's seat, and he put the key in the ignition, turned it slowly, and waited to see what would happen. The engine hummed as the car started up, but otherwise, nothing. No horn, no lights. Jeremy got directions up on his phone and drove off to the address Peter had given him.

As they drove, evening turned to night, and the road became pitch-black. Jeremy had no choice but to turn on the lights and hope nothing strange happened. Thankfully, they did nothing more than illuminate the road ahead.

When they finally arrived at the address they were given, they saw a church. It was completely dark, save for the white sedan's headlights on the building. Jeremy pulled the gun out of the glove compartment, where he'd put it before taking off, and held it one hand while taking Susan's hand in the other. They exchanged a look, both terrified for their safety. That they didn't see or hear a single other sign of life only heightened their anxiety.

The couple got out of the sedan and made their way slowly to the church, their minds flooded with worries of what was to come. They were just about to make it to the front door when they heard a creak. They turned to the side door, Susan's hand over her mouth and Jeremy's gun pointed at the door, and they both breathed out sighs of relief when they saw it was only Peter. His familiar face provided some comfort, but the eerie atmosphere of the dark church and the unanswered questions kept them on edge.

Jeremy called out, "Peter, what's going on? Why did you bring us to this place in the middle of the night?" Peter approached them, his hands raised and his expression serious.

"I'm sorry for the secrecy, but I had no choice. There's something important I need to show you, something that could change everything. But first, you need to promise me you'll keep this confidential, no matter what you see inside."

Susan nodded hesitantly and said, "We're here for you, Peter, but we need to know what's happening."

"It'll be easier if I show you," he replied. Peter motioned for them to follow him into the church, and they reluctantly joined him at the side door. He walked through and held it open for them to pass. As they stepped into the darkness of the church, they couldn't help but wonder whether their trust in Peter would prove misplaced in the end.

Inside, there were over a hundred people sitting in total silence. Jeremy and Susan regarded them with apprehension as Peter led them past the pews. The only sound was that of their footsteps, which further unsettled the couple. They passed rows and rows of people, all dead silent, until they reached the front. Peter stood before the congregation, took a deep breath, and then addressed them in a hushed tone, as if afraid of being overheard by someone or something.

"Thank you all for being here tonight," he began. "I know this may seem strange and frightening, but I assure you, it's necessary. We've gathered here because we've discovered something that could change the course of our lives, and possibly the world."

The tension in the room was palpable, and Jeremy and Susan exchanged worried glances. What could be so important that it required such secrecy and so many people?

Peter continued, "Deep within the archives of this very church, we've unearthed a set of ancient manuscripts. These manuscripts hold knowledge that the world has been unaware of for centuries. Knowledge that has the potential to bring about a new era of understanding and unity."

The congregation kept silent.

Peter's voice trembled with excitement as he said, "These manuscripts reveal the existence of a long-forgotten civilization that possessed advanced technology and wisdom far beyond our comprehension. They offer a glimpse into a lost world of wonders, and we believe that it's time to share this knowledge with the world."

Jeremy and Susan stared at him; both their eyes were wide with fascination. The mystery was deepening, and they couldn't deny their curiosity about what these ancient manuscripts contained.

"But," Peter continued, "there are powerful forces that would stop at nothing to keep this knowledge hidden. That's why we've gathered here tonight, in secrecy, to discuss our plan to share this discovery with the world and ensure that it doesn't fall into the wrong hands."

As Peter's words hung in the air, Jeremy could not help himself; he had to ask.

"Peter, what in the world are you talking about? What does it have to do with the crazy black sedan?"

Peter's eyes met Jeremy's, and for a moment, there was a hint of hesitation in his expression. He had only revealed part of the story, and Jeremy's question hit a nerve.

"The black sedan," Peter began slowly, "is part of the puzzle. It's connected to the people who want to keep this knowledge hidden. They've been tracking us, and that's why we had to be so secretive about our meeting here tonight."

"Peter, you're not giving us the full picture. What people are after this knowledge, and why is it so important?" Susan asked, emboldened by the deepening mystery.

"The people after this knowledge are part of a shadowy organization, one that has controlled hidden truths throughout history. They believe that the world isn't ready for the revelations in the manuscripts, and they'll stop at nothing to keep them hidden."

Jeremy's mind raced as he processed the information. This was far more complex and dangerous than he had ever imagined.

"So, what's our role in all of this, Peter? Why did you get us involved?"

Peter looked at them both, his gaze steady and resolute.

"You two are my most trusted friends. I brought you here because I need your help to protect and share this knowledge. We're going to form a group, a network of individuals who believe in the importance of revealing these secrets to the world. All of us gathered here will be part of that group. But it won't be easy. They will hunt, chase, and test us. Are you willing to be a part of this?"

Jeremy and Susan exchanged a glance once more, this time with a sense of determination. They knew they were entering a world of secrecy, danger, and intrigue, but the lure of hidden knowledge and the possibility of making a positive impact on the world was too enticing to resist.

"Peter, what is this knowledge?" Jeremy asked.

"We do not exist," he replied simply.

"What do you mean, we do not exist?" Pressed Jeremy.

Peter's expression grew even more serious, and he spoke slowly. He seemed to choose his words with care.

"I mean that the information within those ancient manuscripts challenges our very understanding of reality. It suggests that the world as we know it, the systems, institutions and even our identities, are part of a carefully constructed illusion. The manuscripts propose we are all living in a false reality, one that forces have shaped and controlled beyond our comprehension."

"You're saying that everything we believe about ourselves, and our world, is a lie?" Susan asked. Peter nodded solemnly.

"Yes, that's the essence of it. These manuscripts detail a different truth, one that they have kept us from discovering. It's a reality that could change everything, and that's why it's so crucial that we protect and share this knowledge."

Sundry thoughts ran through Jeremy's overtaxed mind, a mix of fascination and disbelief. The implications of what Peter was saying were staggering.

"But how do we even unravel this? And who are the people trying to stop us?"

"Unravelling this mystery and confronting those who seek to suppress it won't be easy. But we have allies, individuals who have dedicated their lives to understanding the truth. As for our adversaries, they are a powerful and enigmatic organization known as 'The Veil.' They have operated in the shadows for centuries, ensuring that the world remains in its current state of ignorance."

The gravity of their situation weighed heavily on Jeremy and Susan. They were going to be part of something far larger and more profound than they could have ever imagined, a battle between hidden knowledge and a carefully crafted illusion.

"But what does it have to do with the black sedan?" Jeremy asked. Susan nodded. They were still curious about that piece of the puzzle.

"Oh that," said Peter with a smile on his face, looking more relaxed than he had all night. "That was a malfunctioning car I needed to take back to the dealership for work under warranty. I hope it added a bit of excitement to your day. Is the car parked at your place still? I need it next week."

Jeremy nodded, satisfied with the answer. He then looked at Susan, the severity in his gaze showing a resolve to do what must be done. She nodded in agreement, as if she could read his mind and see his exact intentions. Then Jeremy took out the Smith & Wesson and shot Peter in the head, killing him instantaneously.

The previously silent church was filled with noise. Cries of panic and despair echoed through the vast space, and the thudding of footsteps and creaking of wood joined the voices as people shot out of their seats and made for the exits. Two burly men rushed at Jeremy, but he took them down quickly with two well-placed shots to the skull. The other hundred or so individuals poured out of the church, none of them brave or foolish enough to risk their lives for this. They ran into the woods, disappearing into the night's shadow.

Jeremy and Susan walked out and headed back to the white sedan. When they reached it, Susan pulled out her mobile and punched a few numbers.

"It is done," she said once the call went through.

The voice on the other end simply replied: "The Committee of the Veil knows we can depend on our best and most trusted members. Thank you." Then the line went dead. Susan put her phone away and looked at Jeremy, a satisfied grin on her face.

"The Committee is happy with our work, and guess what? It looks like we get to keep our new car."

A Celestial Sweep

In the vast expanse of the universe, there are many planets and galaxies. As you can imagine, they produce staggering amounts of garbage.

To make sure the universe stays tidy, there is an extraordinary cleaning company called 'Cosmic Cleaners.' Its motto is: *Bringing Cosmic Clarity to the Universe, One Celestial Sweep at a Time!*

The company was contracted eons ago, so long ago no one really remembers who requested the service to pick up space debris and keep the galaxies clean. Each year, the invoice goes out and gets paid, and so the company continues its service.

The company has seen everything from shattered asteroids to rogue comets, but nothing prepared them for the shocking sight that awaited them when they approached the third planet from a modest star.

Captain Stella Argyle piloted the advanced spacecraft, the *Starbright*, through the endless void of space to fulfill their contract. The ship was equipped with state-of-the-art vacuum technology capable of scooping up celestial clutter with unmatched precision.

As the captain approached the blue and green planet, third from the bright star, she noticed the sensors going haywire. The screens lit up with blinking lights and the alarms blared. Captain Stella couldn't believe her eyes. The space around this planet was littered with a dazzling display of discarded satellites, defunct rockets, and abandoned space junk. It was a cosmic graveyard of technological relics.

"Good galaxies! Look at this mess!" Stella exclaimed, her purple skin paling with shock. "I've seen nothing like it!"

Her loyal crew, consisting of diverse alien species from all corners of the universe, gazed in disbelief at the spectacle before them. Each satellite that floated past their ship told a story of ingenuity and exploration, but now they were nothing more than lifeless, abandoned relics.

Stella adjusted her control panel and transmitted a message to her crew. "Alright team, it's time to put our cosmic cleaning skills to the test. Let's tidy up this space junk and give this planet a fresh start."

The crew jumped into action. They deployed a fleet of smaller cleaning drones equipped with powerful suction beams, each one resembling a mini absorber cleaner. With expert precision, they scooped up the derelict satellites and defunct rockets, depositing them into the ship's storage compartments.

The hours turned into days and the days into weeks, and all the while, the crew continued to work tirelessly. They navigated the debris field with care, avoiding collisions with the millions of discarded objects. They marvelled at the variety of satellites they encountered, from communication satellites to long-forgotten scientific instruments.

While they cleaned, they couldn't help but wonder about the story behind each piece of debris' journey into space. The sheer number and variety of abandoned inventions was a testament to the curiosity and innovation of the planet's inhabitants, but it was also a stark reminder of the need for responsible stewardship of the cosmos.

Finally, after weeks of diligent work, the crew had cleared the space around the planet. The once-cluttered orbit was now unmarred by debris, revealing the pristine beauty of the cosmos. The planet's atmosphere could be seen clearly, free of the remnants of past space clutter.

Captain Stella gazed out at the planet below, a tear of pride in her eye. "This planet looks magnificent once more," she said. "Let this be a reminder to all crew members that our job is a noble endeavour. But let us also remind our friends and family that with great technological innovation comes the responsibility to care for the celestial playground we share."

With their mission accomplished, the Cosmic Cleaners bid farewell to the planet and continued their journey through the universe, ever vigilant in their mission to keep the cosmos clean and beautiful.

Meanwhile, on that third planet from the bright star, humanity was wondering what had happened.

Over the past few weeks, all the planet's traffic was slowly grinding to a halt. As the governments of the world scrambled to figure out what was happening, each fearing a terror attack or aggression from a foreign power, the planet's GPS systems completely fizzled out. The world economy shut down, and panic hit the share markets, causing a crash that would turn into a recession and then a depression. The weapons systems of every single country went down, and their governments scrambled to find out who was responsible—but they had no means of doing so and could not retaliate against their suspected enemies. They were left disarmed and completely in the dark.

On the night side of the planet, Milly Sanderson and her daughter were out looking at the night sky. Her daughter pointed to the night sky and said: "Mum, look how clear the night is. No clutter. I wonder what happened?"

"Well, sweetie, I guess someone just did a celestial sweep and cleaned up," Milly replied.

You

In silence deep, I reside alone,

My heart beats in rhythm all its own.

Do I have atrial fibrillation? No!

But in the stillness of my inner night,

I can hear my heart's call for love's light.

In shadows cast, my soul remains confined, looking for love.

A world of quiet, in the deaf and blind,

My heart's desire, a whisper, far and faint.

Longing for one with whom to acquaint.

My ears are not deaf to love's sweet serenade,

A melody that should never fade,

Yet in my chest, a yearning's constant plea,

A heart that longs for love's symphony.

Though stars above may shine in a brilliant gleam,

And moonlight dance on a tranquil stream.

Within my breast, no darkness shrouds my soul.

My heart's true yearning, I cannot control.

In every touch, in every gentle breeze,

Love's calling cards, I shall never fail to seize,

For though I long for warmth in love's embrace,

My heart's desire is lost in empty space.

When you are not near me.

I wander through the world, a lonesome ghost,

In search of love, until I find the one I need the most,

You, my Red!

Best Friends

In the quiet village of Glenwood, New South Wales, there lived three inseparable friends: Joe, Ed, and Martin. They had known each other since childhood. They grew up together in the orphanage, and their bond was unbreakable.

The years passed, and the trio remained friends. Each of them kept in touch and they all continue to live in Glenwood, the perfect small village. It was good to them when they were in the orphanage, and now, with their own families, they could not see any reason to leave. They had become an important part of the Glenwood ecosystem, and the village adored them.

As close as they were, the three friends were very different people, with distinct personalities that made them stand out in the village. Joe was the eccentric dreamer. He owned the local bookstore, which was always running specials that delighted his customers. They loved the book sales and specials and always enjoyed Joe's take on the most recent bestseller. This month, it was J. F. Nodar's *The Universe Between Us*. Joe loved his customers, and they loved him back. Joe never married but was sure his soulmate was out there, somewhere, just waiting for him.

Ed was the level-headed realist. He went into banking and ran the local branch of the national bank. He was married, with a lovely stay-at-home wife and three children.

Martin was the charismatic charmer of the group. With a knack for sales and mechanics, he ran the largest auto dealership in the state. Also married, Martin had one daughter, who he doted on.

One summer evening, when the three friends gathered at Joe's place on the lake, their lives took an unexpected turn. The village was buzzing with excitement because a meteor shower was forecasted. Ed and Martin had no interest in watching the night show in the sky, so they spent the evening at Joe's. However, their dreamer friend, his head perennially up in the clouds, wanted to see the rare celestial event. As a compromise, they watched it on Joe's back deck with a keg of beer.

The three friends watched in awe as the meteors streaked across the night sky. Even Ed and Martin had to admit that it was spectacular, even if it was mostly the booze talking. Then one of the meteors veered off course and landed with a thud just a few yards from their spot. The impact created a small crater and sent a shockwave through the air, knocking the friends off their feet.

Shaken but curious, they cautiously approached the crater. To their amazement, they found an unusual-looking rock in the center. It was giving off an otherworldly glow. Joe couldn't resist picking it up.

"This is incredible!" He exclaimed, holding the glowing rock. "Imagine what this could be!"

Ed, ever the realist, was cynical. "Joe, it's just a meteorite. I'm sure scientists will study it, categorize it, and we'll forget all about it soon."

Martin just took a sip of his beer and just walked back to the deck.

But Joe had a different idea. He couldn't help but feel an unusual connection with the rock, as if it had whispered some ancient secrets into his mind. That night, after his friends left for the night, he couldn't sleep. He stayed up and wandered back to the crater. The meteor kept glowing. Joe was mesmerized; he felt like he could stare at it all night long. However, his biological needs ultimately won out. After a few hours of staring at the meteor and absorbing its glow, Joe eventually got sleepy, and had to admit that he couldn't spend the night outside in front of the crater unless he wanted to sleep on the hard ground. Reluctantly, he left the beautiful, brilliant meteorite where it was and went to bed. He'd come back to it in the morning.

Joe had only gotten a few hours of sleep when a series of loud banging noises woke him up. Groggy and bleary-eyed, he looked around in confusion, trying to figure out if he was still dreaming. He'd been having a recurring dream of watching the meteorite land, feeling the impact run up his entire body with a rhythmic thrum. As he tried to get his bearings, he heard the loud noises again, and realised that someone was knocking on his door.

Upon answering the door, Joe found that the Australian military had showed up outside his house. A general asked him about the meteorite and, of course, Joe took him down to the crater. It was still there but was no longer glowing.

Military scientists told Joe to stay back, put on protective equipment, and whisked the meteorite away. The general in charge told Joe not to tell anyone they had been there and left. He felt as if he was in a daze while all of this happened. All he could think of was the glowing meteorite, even after it was long gone.

In the days that followed, Joe's demeanour changed. He called his assistant manager at the bookstore to let her know he was taking a few days off. He entrusted her with the opening and closing of the store. However, Joe did not go on vacation. He sat at home all day, reading through every single book in his prodigious home library that he hadn't read already. In two days, he devoured over 1,000 books. He could not tell if he had slept or ate. He needed information. More and more information.

Once he ran out of books at home, Joe went to the Glenwood library. He found a corner of the extensive library and started reading.

He did not stop.

Physics, languages, chemistry, history, biology, mathematics, quantum mechanics, string theory, geology, art, religion, no subject was too great for him to wrap his increasingly voracious mind around. When Joe finished all the books in the local library, he went to the NSW state library and devoured all the books there, too.

After that, he read through every single book in every single major university in Sydney.

Joe was suddenly a fountain of wisdom, astonishing himself and others with his newfound brilliance. He could solve complex math problems with ease, speak fluently in multiple languages, and understand the intricacies of science, technology, and history. He had become an accidental genius.

The town was abuzz with talk of Joe's transformation. They sought his guidance on various matters, and he was never at a loss for answers. He helped the local farmers improve their crop yields, tutored the town's children in their studies, and even provided insights on renewable energy that baffled scientists and the local government.

Joe's wisdom was not just limited to Glenwood. News of his incredible knowledge had spread far and wide, and people from all over the world sought his counsel. Soon, world leaders and scholars were knocking at his door, hoping to benefit from his newfound intellect. Universities started buying land in Glenwood to build new centres of knowledge in all the sciences and arts.

All because of Joe.

In the end, the small village of Glenwood became renowned as the home of the humble bookshop owner-turned genius. He had transformed the ordinary village into a global centre of knowledge.

Ed and Martin watched in awe as their friend's life took an extraordinary turn. They couldn't help but be proud of him, though it meant they were spending less time together. The bonds of their friendship remained unbreakable, even though Joe was now busy solving global problems.

One day, Joe invited his friends to his lake house. Both Ed and Martin were happy for the invite, as they had spent no time with Joe in the last few months. When they arrived, they saw Joe smiling at them, holding up three large mugs of beer. He looked no different from the man they'd known months ago, before the meteorite fell in front of his house.

They greeted each other, gave a quick toast, and then sat down to watch the small waves in the lake. The three friends drank in silence until Martin commented: "Well Joe, you sure got famous."

Both Ed and Joe laughed at that.

"I guess I did. It seems the world can't get enough of me now," Joe replied.

"What's next for you, Joe?" Ed asked. Joe had been smiling the whole time, just happy to be with his friends again, but at this question his expression changed. His smile fell, and he stared pensively at the surface of the water, diligently avoiding eye contact with his friends. He took a long swig of beer as if to delay answering the question.

"I'm going away, guys. That's what's next for me," he said at last.

"Figures. You saved the environment in Glenwood, why not elsewhere? Where are you off to? Europe? The US?" Martin asked.

"No. Not really," was Joe's mysterious answer.

"Joe, you sound odd. If not Europe or the US, then where?" Pressed Ed. He and Martin were worried now. Joe always had lofty ideas of where life would take him, but he never failed to share them. He never danced around his aspirations or gave cryptic answers. Now, instead of answering, he took another sip of his beer, and with his right index finger pointed to the heavens. Both friends looked up and saw nothing but stars and wondered if Joe had lost it.

"What do you mean by, uh..." Ed pointed his own index finger to the sky.

"I leave tonight. I'm being picked up."

"Who's picking you up, Joe?" Asked Martin.

"Zillgot," was all Joe said.

"Zillgot? Who in the world is *Zillgot*?" Asked Ed.

"Zillgot is from Proxima Centauri b."

"Proxima Centauri b? What are you saying, Joe? That this Zillgot is an alien?" Ed asked again.

"Yes, I am. Zillgot is from Proxima Centauri b, four light-years away. It is our closest known exoplanet neighbour. Proxima b is a super Earth exoplanet that orbits an M-type star. It should be fun living there," Joe answered. He spoke nonchalantly, as if he was answering a question about the weather or where he bought his socks.

"Fun? What do you mean by *fun*? No one has ever gone farther than the moon, and you expect us to believe you're going four years from Earth?"

"It's four light-years way, not four years. There's a difference. Do you want me to tell you the difference, Martin?"

"No smarty pants, I don't. I just don't get how you can say this stuff like it's no big deal, talking about *Zillgot* from Proxima Centauri b coming to whisk you four light-years away. It is a big deal. It's nuts!"

"Martin, calm down. It's for the best. I have exhausted my capacity to learn from and convey information to Earth citizens. I must enhance my thinking abilities. I need more information, more knowledge. Much more."

"What do you mean by that, Joe? What information do you need? Why do you need it?"

Joe paused before responding. He needed to find the right words to explain his situation to his best friends. He desperately needed them to understand.

"My mind is like a supercomputer. I'm learning and harnessing the power of multiple interconnected processing cores. My mind is using an immense amount of energy, generating over 30 megawatts a day. Do you realise how much that is? 30 megawatts a day could power a small city. My mind is a tool, a powerful one, and I can't use it solely to benefit Earth. There are other civilizations that need me."

Martin and Ed looked at each other, eyes wide in incredulity. Then, they burst out laughing.

"Oh, you had us there for a moment, Joe," said Ed, slapping his knee and stifling more laughter.

"Yeah, 30 megawatts. More power to more civilizations. Funny." Martin gave Joe a playful punch in the shoulder. He just shook his head. He hadn't gotten through to them. He wished he had more time, but looking down at his watch, he saw that there was precious little remaining. He would leave soon. He just hoped that Ed and Martin would one day understand.

"Zillgot should be here any minute. I'm sorry I can't stay longer, but I'll miss you both. I'll never forget your friendship. It means more to me than words can say."

"Yeah, love you too, buddy. You can knock it off now," Martin said, still chuckling.

"Which one's your ride? Maybe that cloud over there?" Ed asked jokingly, pointing to a lazily drifting cloud resembling a saucer. Joe shook his head and pointed to the opposite end of the horizon.

"My ride's over there." Ed and Martin turned to look, and they nearly dropped their beers when they beheld a true spaceship, saucer-like, hurtling towards them. Once its shadow loomed above them, blocking out the sun, it stopped. They watched in awe and fear as it hovered eerily over their heads.

The spacecraft was a gleaming, metallic disc with a perfectly smooth surface that appeared almost seamless. Its edges were marked by a soft, faintly pulsating blue light. It was an otherworldly technological marvel, like nothing Ed and Martin had seen before and would ever see again.

The flying saucer emitted no sound. It was frighteningly silent as it defied the laws of physics. It maintained a steady distance above Joe's head, suspended by some kind of advanced anti-gravity technology. Martin and Ed, with slack jaws and wide eyes, were illuminated by the mysterious glow emanating from the craft. Joe's features reflected a mix of curiosity and wonder, but not a touch of fear. He was ready for his ride, even if his dear friends were not.

Its gentle bluish light shone down on Joe in a beam, like a ray from the sun, creating intriguing shadows and highlights on his face and body. They coalesced around him, enveloping him completely, and once the light faded, along with the shadows and highlights, he was gone. The ship wasted no time in taking off, disappearing up into the clouds and beyond the horizon.

Ed and Martin stared at the last place they had seen the spacecraft. Their eyes didn't leave the spot for what felt like hours, as they tried to process what they'd seen. Joe wasn't joking. He hadn't lost it. He'd been different ever since that meteorite landed in front of his house, and this was the result. He was off to save civilizations that Ed and Martin would never know. When they finally looked away from the sky and at each other, they both had the same thought: *Who would have thought that a rock would turn Joe into a genius?*

Martin and Ed sat back on the deck, opened two more beers, and realised that they weren't sad to lose their friend—because they hadn't lost him at all. He would never forget them, and they would never forget him. Joe, Ed, and Martin were, and always would be, best friends. It didn't matter how many light-years apart they were; nothing would change that.

Lesson # 23 – How to Support Your Wife

My wife Isabel had always been a free spirit at heart.

From her eclectic taste in music to her adventurous palate, she embraced life with an open mind. But there was one thing that had always made her feel confined, one tiny piece of fabric that symbolized societal norms and expectations—her bra.

One sunny Saturday morning, as she stood in front of her closet, she felt a surge of rebellion. She had spent her entire life obeying the unspoken rule that a woman should always wear a bra when outside the comfort of her home. But today, she decided, was going to be different. Today, she wanted to feel the liberation of going braless.

Isabel selected a flowy, bohemian dress from her wardrobe, the perfect outfit for her plan. As she slipped into it and admired herself in the mirror, she took a deep breath. The sunlight streaming through her bedroom window bathed her in warmth and courage. With a resolute smile, she left her bedroom, leaving her bra behind, and descended the stairs.

I was in the kitchen brewing our morning coffee, and as Isabel entered the room, my eyes widened in surprise. The dress was modest, but it lacked the supportive undergarment that had been a constant in her wardrobe for years.

"Isabel. You're not wearing a bra."

She grinned, her heart pounding with excitement. "I know, James. Today, I want to feel free, just for a change."

I smiled, set down the coffeepot, and walked over to wrap her in an embrace.

"You know you're beautiful whether or not you're wearing a bra, right?

"I know James. You tell me that every day and I love you for it."

"Is there another dress that might provide you with more support, so you don't have to wear a bra?"

"Not really. That's why I choose this flowy dress. You like it?"

I did like the dress, but I was worried about the police. I was going to say so, but Isabel's phone rang before I could get the words out. She looked at the ID and said: "It's Mum. Is it OK if I take it? She doesn't do quick phone calls so it might be a while, but we can go to the mall after. Is that alright?"

"Of course, sweetie, go ahead. I'll keep busy."

After Isabel stepped out of the kitchen and onto the patio, I ran to our home office, powered up the computer and typed in: *can a woman go braless in New South Wales, Australia?*

I got 10,300,000 responses in 0.49 seconds. Right away, I saw what I was looking for. The laws around female toplessness in NSW were not what I expected.

The law in New South Wales describes obscene exposure as an offence that can prohibit certain acts of public nudity, depending on the circumstances. Fox example, it is an offence under section 5 of the Summary Offences Act 1988 (NSW), and it carries a maximum penalty of 6 months in prison and/or a fine of 10 penalty units or $110 per unit. I read the maximum could be $1,100.

To establish the offence, the state of NSW would have to prove beyond reasonable doubt that Isabel was in or within view of a public place or school, or that she obscenely exposed herself and did so willfully.

I read further and clarified what was considered a 'public place.' Unsurprisingly, it's a place or part of a premise that is open to, or used by the public, whether for payment, and whether only open to a limited class of persons. I'm not a lawyer, but I'd say that shopping centres, restaurants, pubs and clubs, and sporting venues would be included in this definition.

That left me to ponder:

What falls under the category of 'obscene' and 'willful'?

I researched further, and found that depending on the factual circumstances, the magistrate decides whether something is 'obscene' on a case-by-case basis, while 'willful' refers to intentional actions.

Well, Isabel was intent on going braless, and if they brought her in front of a magistrate, she could get fined up to $1,100 depending on the magistrate's mood.

I heard Isabel's footsteps growing closer to the office, and I quickly minimised the screen before she could see my research.

"Sorry it took so long. You know my mum; she'll talk about anything under the sun till her voice gives out. Anyway, are you ready to go?"

"Let me turn off the computer," I said. I shut it off and then turned back to Isabel. She looked so liberated without her bra, and I didn't want to ruin her happiness, but I felt I should at least warn her before we went out. I doubted either of us wanted our day out to be interrupted by a run-in with law enforcement.

"Sweetie, you know you could get in trouble if it offends someone when they see you braless?"

"I know, James, but imagine having a metalworking vise around your genitals for hours. How would you feel?"

I gave this comparison a ponder. It was quite effective.

"Isabel, I need to go change. Give me five minutes?"

"James, you look fantastic. Why do you need to change?"

"Just give me five-minutes. Be back soon."

Taking two steps at the time up the staircase, I rushed to our bedroom and took care of business. In less than five minutes, I was back, grabbing the car's keys and motioning to Isabel that we were ready to go.

As I backed out of the garage and shifted into drive, Isabel asked: "James, why did you go back upstairs? You changed nothing. You're wearing the same clothes as before."

"Isabel, how long have we been married?"

"24 years, darling. Why, are you worried I forgot?" She asked teasingly. I let out a chuckle.

"No, neither of us are old enough to start getting senile. But all those years together have taught me so much, and this morning, I learnt something new."

"What did you learn?"

I shift my bottom a bit to make myself more comfortable before answering my wife.

"Isabel, I just added lesson #23 to my list."

"Lesson #23. What's that?"

"Lesson #23 is how to support your wife."

"I see, James, and how are you supporting me?"

"Well, I'm coming with you to the mall, and I'm going commando."

Lemons

Northport, New South Wales is a quaint, small village about 85 kilometres south of Sydney. Here lived a man named John Bosco, who was, without a doubt, the unluckiest homeowner in the world. His misfortunes started when a freak accident involving a runaway hot-air balloon obliterated his house. Then, a series of bizarre events unfolded: a flock of seagulls repeatedly dive-bombed his car, a stray llama camped out in his backyard and gave birth to a whole herd of babies, and a magical toilet in his house took up a sudden interest in playing the bagpipes.

The straw that broke the camel's back was when a swarm of bees set up shop in his lounge area. This incident forced John to take time away from his job to sort it all out. When he came back, he found that he'd missed too many days and was fired.

Without a job, he couldn't make his mortgage payments to the bank, so the bank worked with him on his repayments. Alas, John could not even put a single cent towards his mortgage, and the bank was soon ready to foreclose and evict him.

John was at his wit's end. He had no solutions, no clever tricks, no sudden influx of money from a recently deceased, incredibly wealthy relative. He had no choice, it seemed, but to face eviction. He stood in front of his ruined home, drenched in honey (from the aforementioned bees), confronting the grim reality that he would soon be homeless. At that very moment, however, his phone rang, and it was none other than his old university buddy, Dave, notorious for making deals of all kinds. The rumour while at the university was that Dave was the Devil's assistant. Of course, this was not true, but the rumour persisted.

"Hey, John," Dave said with a mischievous chuckle. "I heard you're in a bit of a pickle. Need some help?"

John, desperate and honey-soaked, sighed. "A 'pickle' is a huge understatement. I'm about to lose my house and I have no clue what to do about it."

"Not to worry, my friend!" Dave exclaimed. "I know a guy who can help you out, no problem. Just one little thing—you have to sign a contract with him, and he'll get you out of your mess *only* if the contract is upheld. Understood?"

"What kind of contract?" John asked cautiously. He remembered the rumours at uni. Dave pulling stunts like this was exactly how they got started.

"Oh, it's just a standard contract. The contract includes what I expect from you and any penalties for breach or incomplete contract provisions. You know, the usual stuff, just run-of-the-mill."

John hesitated for a moment, but asked: "Dave, have any of your friends had any dealings with your guy? How has that worked out for them? Can he really help?"

Dave laughed loudly.

"John, do you remember when I helped Robert Bailey pass his physics test, back in uni? What about Elizabeth Arnold? Remember when she won Miss Congeniality in her last year, just like she wanted? If you need more examples, I can go on. We might be here a while."

Dave's comment gave John pause. As shady as he was, John remembered Robert and Elizabeth, along with several other fellow students who achieved their university aspirations and goals with 'help' from Dave. Maybe, just maybe, Dave could help him too. At the very least, John could meet with this mysterious contact of his and decide then.

"OK, Dave, let's do it. Arrange a meeting with your guy."

"Excellent." answered Dave. He arranged a meeting at a nearby park under the shade of a twisted, gnarled tree. *A perfect spot for a devilish rendezvous*, Dave thought to himself.

John, ever punctual, showed up right on time, approaching the tree nervously. For the umpteenth time, he wondered why they couldn't just meet at a coffee shop like normal people.

Once John was standing beneath the gnarled branches, the ground shook and a plume of smoke swirled around him. Suddenly, Dave's guy materialized before him, dressed in a sharp suit and a fiery red tie, with a big, mischievous smile on his face.

"John, allow me to introduce myself. My name is D. D. Cifarelli." His voice was booming. "I hear from my assistant Dave that you need some help. What's the problem?"

John, feeling uneasy, explained his predicament, and Mr Cifarelli, who was in a rather pleasant mood, said, "I can help you, but in return, I have a contract for you to sign. This contract states you must retrieve for me three items: a unicorn's horn, a dragon's scale, and a fairy's laugh. You must procure these items in three days, as per the contract. Once you have completed the assignment, we shall back here in the park, say at 6 PM?"

John gulped. He'd never been more certain that the rumours about Dave had been true. He was terrified about what secret provisions might lurk in a contract drawn up by this man, but if he didn't sign, he'd be out on his behind without a roof over his head or a pot to piss in. There wasn't much else he had to lose. He had no choice.

"OK, fine. I'll sign. But how do I even find these things?"

"First things first, here is the contract," the dapper man said, handing John two sets of the same contract. John signed both and returned them to Mr Cifarelli, showing that he did not need his copy. The man raised an eyebrow in surprise.

"You did not read it? That is never a wise thing to do when entering a contact."

"Look Mr Cifarelli, I'm desperate. I already have nothing; what more could go wrong? Now, tell me how to find those things you mentioned so I can get this over with."

Mr Cifarelli smiled and handed John a small, enchanted compass.

"This compass will guide you to each item. It's quite simple. The compass will lead you to the most unlikely places, but remember, you have just three days to collect them all."

Mr Cifarelli smiled and, in a puff of smoke, vanished completely, leaving John totally flabbergasted and alone beneath the tree.

With the magical compass in hand, John immediately set off on his quest. The compass, as Mr Cifarelli said, led him to the most unlikely places. He entered realms beyond his comprehension and saw things he thought only existed in films and storybooks. He encountered strange, mystical creatures; it took him a few tries, but John learned to negotiate with a unicorn, brave the fiery breath of a dragon, and, after an extraordinary amount of trial and error, extract a fairy's laugh.

Finally, on the third day, John returned to the park at 6:05 PM. John hated being late, but he couldn't help it, for there had been a traffic jam on Main Street. Mr Cifarelli was there waiting for him, and John proudly presented him with the unicorn's horn, the dragon's scale, and the fairy's laugh.

"I am impressed, John. Very impressed," he said. And true to his word, he snapped his fingers and restored John's house and his bank account to their former glory.

"Enjoy the house and everything that comes your way, John," Mr Cifarelli said cryptically. Before John could ask what that mean, he let out a raucous cackle and evaporated into thin air.

When John returned to his newly restored home and stepped through the pristine threshold, he couldn't help but chuckle. He had been on a wild ride. Encountering the impossible and dealing with Mr Cifarelli was, in retrospect, an easy feat. Sure, unicorns and dragons and fairies were real, and there were all sorts of magic in the world and the worlds beyond, but it wasn't of the Devil. How could it be? John had gotten what he wanted with no strings attached. No last-minute take backs, no sneaky revelations about some clause in the contract that stipulated the relinquishing of John's eternal soul. Whatever Dave did while at university was just good management of circumstances. Mr Cifarelli was just a strange, mystical individual. After the past three days, John could almost take the mystical for granted.

He was not the devil; that would be silly.

John was ecstatic. He had truly learned the meaning of the saying: *when life gives you lemons, make a lemonade.* Or rather, make a deal that gets you ahead.

From that day forward, John was happy in his home. At least, until a week later when Dave knocked on his door. When he opened it, he saw Dave looked stupendous. Better than ever, in fact. He was dressed just as Mr Cifarelli had been, and the new clothes seemed to suit him perfectly.

"Dave, so good to see you. You look terrific. What brings you here?" Dave flashed him a vulpine grin. John's good spirits faltered a bit. There seemed to be something sinister behind that smile.

"Why John, it's your initiation! I've come to collect you so you can start your new position."

"My new position? I don't understand. What are you talking about?"

"John, did you keep the copy of your contract with Mr Cifarelli?"

John shook his head.

"Did you read it before signing it?"

"No," John said nervously. Dave waved his hands, and a large paper appeared in front of him.

"Here is the original contract you signed. It states that if you fail in your endeavour, as per your agreement with Mr Cifarelli, he will relinquish his otherworldly powers, transferring them to his assistant. Then you, in turn, will become the new assistant. It's right here in paragraph 16, section 6." John looked at the paragraph, but his worry was gone. Clearly, there'd been a mistake.

"I hate to break it to you, but you've made a mistake. I didn't fail. I got the unicorn's horn, the dragon's scale, and the fairy's laugh. All by the third day, as agreed. Mr Cifarelli even said he was impressed," John said, puffing out his chest.

"Yes John, you did. And it was very impressive. But you were late. Paragraph 19, section 3 stipulates that you are to arrive at 6 PM on the dot. You arrived at 6:05 PM, thus invoking paragraph 66, section 66."

Like that, all the hot air blew out of John like a deflated balloon. His shoulders sunk and he fell into a slouch. He felt utterly defeated. It wasn't fair. Why hadn't Mr Cifarelli told him about the time? Why did he have to be late on that day, when he had never been late a day in his life?

"So...what happens then?" John asked. To say he was nervous was an understatement. He felt like a boulder had been plopped in his stomach, weighing him down. He wanted nothing less than to hear Dave's answer.

"D. D. Cifarelli stops being the Devil. His current assistant takes over the role, and you now work for me." With that, Dave pushed past John into his newly refurbished house, and strolled to the dining room table. He pulled out a seat and motioned to it chivalrously, indicating to John that it was time to sit and start talking details.

John locked his front door and followed the new Devil, taking his seat. He was deflated, defeated. There was nothing he could do. How could he go against the Devil? He'd signed the contract without looking at it; this could have been avoided if he hadn't been so damn cocky.

John thought back to what he thought he'd learned. It was all wrong. He thought he'd made lemonade from lemons, shrewdly navigating a deal to leave him better off than before. But it was Dave and Cifarelli who had been making lemonade, and he was the one getting squeezed.

Killing My Darling

Peter opens his eyes and notices he is flat on his back. Dust is flying all around him.

The last thing he can remember is falling off a cliff. Lying supine, he sees said cliff towering above him, confirming his recollection. It looks to be over 500 metres high.

Peter gets up and dusts himself off. *How is it I'm alive? I should be dead falling from such a distance.* But he isn't.

First, he looks at the ground, wondering if he landed on something to cushion his fall. Nope. There's just hard earth beneath his feet, as he suspected. Then he scans around for something that he could have used to help break his fall. Maybe he had a jetpack? Climbing gear? Anything was possible, seeing as he'd survived a 500-metre fall. But again, he finds nothing. It's just him, the cliff, and the ground.

Peter closes his eyes and thinks, trying to reason his way to an answer. There must be an explanation. Why was he alive? Who in the world could suffer injury that would lead to certain death and come out of it no worse for wear? How could Peter have defied the laws of physics so flagrantly?

Story.

Peter thinks to every *James Bond* and *Mission Impossible* movie he's ever seen. James Bond, Ethan Hunt, and all those characters should have died several times over. But they lived because the plot required that they live. Perhaps the plot requires that Peter lives.

He's a character in a movie!

No, not a movie. Not enough excitement for a movie. Right now, Peter is just staring at the ground. No action hero spends minutes staring at the ground. Movies are about excitement, stimulation. At least, the movies that involve men falling off cliffs are. There's nothing exciting about this.

But a book? Where *minutes* is just a single word? Where doesn't there need to be high-octane thrills on every page? Now that's more likely. Maybe he's in a book instead. Yes, that must be it. He's in a book. Maybe a novel. Probably a short story.

This is a problem. It means his life is not his own. The author could have him fall off as many cliffs as the readers want. One fall could even kill him. But Peter doesn't want to fall off any more cliffs. He doesn't want the entirety of his life to be the words the author puts on the page. He wants to be able to see the edge of the cliff and turn the other way.

To navigate this predicament and possibly communicate with the author, Peter decides he must go through some tests. The first is a self-exploration of the rules and limitations of this fictional world.

Obviously, he is indestructible, which is good since falling off cliffs can really do some damage. But what else can he do? Does he have superpowers?

Peter runs, but he definitely doesn't have speed like the Flash.

He then tries focusing his eyes on the cliff. No heat vision like Superman.

Peter clearly has some ability or control over his decisions and actions, otherwise he wouldn't have been able to mimic the two DC characters. Or maybe it's just the author making him do these things. He doesn't enjoy thinking about that.

Suddenly a chihuahua walks by and says: "Hello Peter. Wonderful morning for a walk." With that, the little dog continues trotting along.

Oh yes, I am definitely a character in a short story. Chihuahuas do not speak, thinks Peter.

Peter walks about to see what else he can find in this short story, and it doesn't take him long to find more confirmation. As he passes by a large boulder, he turns right and stares directly at a unicorn, a pink one at that.

"Peter, so nice to see you again. It's been a while since we took a ride together. Want to hop on? I'm going to go visit the in-laws," says the friendly pink unicorn.

Another confirmation thinks Peter.

"Are we in a story of some kind?" He asks the unicorn.

"A story? What do you mean?"

"I mean, are we real? Or are we just words on a page?" At this, the unicorn whinnies, which Peter assumes is his way of laughing.

"Oh, come on Peter, you know we are. If you think we're not real, then why hang around? Are you coming for a ride or not?"

"No thanks. I think I'll continue walking about."

"OK dude. See you around," the unicorn says. He flaps his wings and takes off.

Wings? Where did those come from? Pegasi have wings, not unicorns.

What is this author thinking?

As Peter continues his walk, he suddenly leaves the cliff behind. Instead, he is standing in front of a desk with a desktop computer on it and an empty chair. Peter approaches the desk. He can't help himself; he reads what's on the computer screen:

"Peter opens his eyes and notices he is flat on his back. Dust is flying all around him.

The last thing he can remember is falling off a cliff. Lying supine, he sees said cliff towering above him, confirming his recollection. It looks to be over 500 metres high.

Peter gets up and dusts himself off. "*How is it I'm alive? I should be dead falling from such a distance*. But he isn't."

That's all he needs. It's the ultimate confirmation that he is indeed in a short story. He is a character thought up by some berserk novelist, who now controls Peter's every thought and action. Or does he? If he did, how could Peter ever have found out that he's just words on a page?

The only thing Peter can do is contact the writer of the short story. He remembers something about a fourth wall, which is the conceptual barrier between any fictional work and its author and readers. Perhaps he can break it. Peter hurries to the chair, sits down and types on the screen:

"Who are you?"

Peter waits for a few seconds before an answer is typed back.

"This is J. F. Nodar. Who is this?"

Good, I contacted the bloody writer. Now to end this insane venture.

"This is Peter. You know, your character who just fell off a 500-metre cliff and survived."

It takes a few more seconds, but the screen lights up with words again.

"Oh yes, Peter, my favourite character. I did not know you could communicate with me. A delightful way to meet you. Well, sort of. I already know you well, seeing as I created you."

"Mr Nodar, I'm tired of being in your stories. Can you stop including me in all these silly stories of yours?"

"Please call me JF. But I'm not sure if I can stop putting you in my stories. You have been my most profitable character by far. My readers love your adventures and escapades. Are you not happy?"

"No, I'm not. Nothing but tragedy and misery fall on me. You never have me in a comedy or a romantic relationship. I'm always falling off cliffs or getting into other situations that cause me bodily harm. Basically, you typecast me, and I hate it."

"I'm sorry Peter, but you are my golden goose, so to speak, so I can't do as you ask."

"In that case, you leave me no choice."

"What do you mean?"

"If you continue to write me in the same short story, then I will disrupt the narrative and piss off your readers."

"What do you mean by that, Peter?"

"What I mean is that if you write I go left, I'll go right. If you write I'm driving a car, I'll fly a kite instead. See what I mean? I will disrupt your story and your readers will hate me and, in turn, hate you. Soon, they'll stop buying your stories about me altogether. No more golden goose for you. You like that JF?"

"Peter, you're just the words I type on the screen. You can't possibly do that."

"How do you know? I've never tried."

Several moments pass in which there is no activity on the screen. Peter waits for JF's response, a feeling of triumph swelling in his chest. Maybe he doesn't have to submit to JF's control. Maybe he can make his own choices. Maybe, just maybe, he's more than the stories that are told about him. After all, what about his life off the page? What about his life in the imagination of the readers? Surely, there's more to his story than JF writes about. He just has to find it—no, he has to make it.

Then, finally, JF types his reply.

"If you feel that way, Peter, I guess it's best if we finish our collaboration."

"Good. I knew you would understand."

Peter waits for whatever will happen next, imagining the freedom that will come with being able to tell his own story. He hears a slow successive tap, tap, tap, tap, as if JF is typing, but nothing comes up on the screen.

Then, he gets an odd feeling in his feet, like pins and needles. He looks down and notices that they are disappearing.

"JF, what's happening?" Peter types frantically.

"I'm doing what you asked. I'm deleting your character, Peter."

Peter continues to hear the tap, tap, tap, and it increases in speed. Soon, he is almost completely gone and cannot even type an appeal to JF to stop. Moments later, he no longer hears the tap, tap, tap. Then Peter is no longer on the page.

Reclining back on his chair, J. F. Nodar sighs in disappointment at the fact that he just killed his most beloved character. But then again, that's what a good author does: kill his darlings off.

Special Holiday

Sally Michaels cherished her Saturday afternoons sitting outside her favourite cozy little coffee shop tucked away in the heart of Northport, New South Wales. It was her oasis of serenity away from the bustling city where she went into work every day.

The rich aroma of freshly brewed coffee danced through the air. She sipped her cappuccino while reading *The Universe Between Us*, the latest novel by her favourite author, J. F. Nodar. The novel had everything Sally loved in a book: humour, romance, adventure, intrigue. Occasionally, she looked up from the book and glanced out the window, enjoying this wonderful moment she got to spend away from work while the rest of the world passed by.

On this afternoon, as she was engrossed in her novel, she looked up and noticed a man loitering outside. He looked suspicious, with a scruffy beard and shabby clothing. Sally couldn't help but keep a wary eye on him. Perhaps it was just her overactive imagination, but something about his presence seemed unsettling.

As Sally finished her cappuccino, slipped her bookmark into her novel, and prepared to leave the shop, she spotted a black SUV pull up to the kerb. Her heart skipped a beat when a remarkably handsome man stepped out of the vehicle. He was impeccably dressed in a tailored suit, his chiselled features catching the sunlight in a way that was almost ethereal. Sally recognised him immediately; he was the newly elected Premier of New South Wales, Andrew Mitchell. The city had been buzzing with excitement about his election.

Sally couldn't believe her luck. She had voted for him and was a tremendous supporter of his policies. It was rare for her to feel so star struck, but this was a significant moment for her.

However, the idyllic moment took a sharp and unexpected turn. Just as Andrew Mitchell approached the sidewalk to make his way into the coffee shop, the loitering man sprang into action, lunging towards the Premier. It was clear that his intentions were malevolent.

In that split second, instinct took over. Sally, driven by a primal urge to protect the charismatic leader, dived forward, pushing the attacker aside with all her strength. The assailant crashed to the ground, startled, and disoriented by her unexpected intervention.

Sally's heart pounded in her chest as the coffee shop patrons and the Premier's security detail rushed to the scene. They apprehended the attacker, who had been carrying a knife. The threat was neutralized, but the shock still lingered in the air and thrummed through Sally's entire body. She felt as if she had been watching herself act in third person, like someone or something else had taken control of her.

The Premier was surprised; he had not expected the courageous woman to intervene. He expressed his gratitude with a warm smile, and they exchanged a few words. Sally, still in disbelief at her own actions, kept her composure and thanked him for his dedication to the people of New South Wales.

News of the incident spread like wildfire. Sally's heroism became the talk of Northport, and the media couldn't get enough of the story. They plastered her face on newspapers, TV screens and social media. People admired her bravery and quick thinking.

As a token of appreciation, the Premier invited Sally to his office. They spoke at length, and a unique bond formed between them. Sally's life took an unexpected turn as she became more involved in the political scene, using her newfound platform to advocate for the causes she held dear.

In the months that followed, Sally Michaels, the unassuming coffee shop regular, became a local hero and an influential figure in New South Wales—all because she followed her instincts in a single crucial moment. Her ordinary afternoon coffee had transformed her into an extraordinary woman, shaping her future in ways she could never have imagined.

As she sat at her now-reserved table at her favourite coffee shop, Sally wondered why an assassin would have tried something so crazy in broad daylight. The question often came to her in calm moments, when she thought back on what she'd done. She thought to herself: *Why would that man take such a big risk, attempting to assassinate the Premier in broad daylight in front of a crowd of people?*

Meanwhile, Andrew Mitchell finished his morning meeting with his press secretary and a few cabinet ministers. He sat alone in his office. Undisturbed, he took out a strange communication device from his coat pocket.

"Have you eliminated the assassin yet?"

"No Sir, he has too much security. But rest assured, we will reach him before he talks to the authorities.

"You better. I cannot have the invasion plan foiled by one good-hearted patriot. How could he possibly think that by removing me, he would save the human species? Is the armada ready?"

"Yes Sir. It lies behind their moon on the dark side."

"Good. Still undetected by the humans?"

"Yes Sir. Their insignificant rovers cannot see through our cloaking devices. We will be ready to proceed with the invasion on Monday, April 1, 2024, on schedule."

"Excellent. Keep me posted." With that, Andrew Mitchell closed the communicator.

He smiled as he contemplated his incredible fortune. The intervention of a single earth female saved his peoples' plan to conquer the Earth on its peoples' special holiday.

What A Worthless Guarantee

After a gruelling day at work, Billy Stuart groggily returned the next morning. The relentless demands of his job as a financial analyst had left him drained and sleep deprived. As he shuffled into the familiar office building, a sense of exhaustion weighed him down. It never went away, no matter how many coffees he downed.

Billy had worked at Preston Financial Services for the past five years. The only bright spot in his days of drudgery came when he arrived at the office in the morning. Then, he'd greet Betty, the friendly secretary at the front desk. Betty could brighten even the gloomiest day with her warm smile and cheery demeanour. She had seen Billy through thick and thin, from the difficulties of the stock market to the birth of his twin daughters. Their daily interactions had become a comforting routine, something Billy relied on.

But today was different. As he approached Betty's desk, he was met with a sight that sent a chill down his spine. Betty, who had greeted him with a smile every single morning for half a decade, was now looking at him with a blank expression.

"Good morning, Betty," Billy said, trying to shake off his exhaustion with a forced smile.

Betty blinked, her eyes registering confusion. "Good morning," she replied cautiously, her tone lacking its usual friendliness. "Can I help you with something?"

Billy was taken aback. "Betty, it's me, Billy Stuart. You know, the guy who's been working here for five years?"

Betty furrowed her brows, her confusion deepening. "Billy Stuart? I'm sorry, but no one by that name has ever worked here. Are you feeling all right, sir? Do you want me to call for a doctor?"

Billy felt a wave of panic wash over him. He had to be dreaming. This couldn't be happening. He glanced around the office, looking for any signs of recognition from his colleagues. But they all were immersed in their work, oblivious to the bizarre situation unfolding at the front desk.

"No, no, Betty, this isn't a joke," Billy stammered, his voice trembling. "I've been here for five years. I sit at the desk near the window on the sixth floor. You say, 'good morning' to me every day."

Betty's expression remained unchanged, and her eyes never left Billy's face. "I'm sorry, sir, but you must be mistaken. I've been working here for ten years, and I've never seen you before."

Billy's mind raced, trying to make sense of the impossible. Had he been erased from the company's history overnight? Was this some elaborate prank? He stumbled away from Betty's desk, his heart pounding in his chest.

Desperate for answers, he rushed to his cubicle on the sixth floor. He dashed to where his desk was, only to find that the space was completely empty, as if no one had ever worked there. He scanned the office for familiar faces, hoping to find someone who recognised him, but no one did. It was as if he had never existed within the walls of Preston Financial Services. People were now looking at him suspiciously, and a few picked up their phones and started making calls.

Billy's thoughts swirled in a chaotic whirlwind as he contemplated his next steps. He couldn't just accept that his entire existence in the company had been erased. He needed to find out what was happening, and he needed to do it fast.

Billy kept looking around the office. He'd been fixated on finding his desk, so he hadn't noticed before, but it was a far cry from the space he was in yesterday. The once-familiar office had transformed into an alien landscape, and Billy felt like an intruder in his own life. Suddenly he heard a voice: "Sir, please come with us."

Billy turned around to see two burly security guards approaching him.

"We need you to leave the premises. Please come with us before we have to call the police," one of the security guards said.

"Wait! I need to see Tom Freston, the president of Preston Financial Services. He'll straighten this whole mess up."

The other security guy pointed in the direction of a glass office and asked: "You mean him?"

Billy followed where the guard pointed and saw a complete stranger. At first he thought he was looking in the wrong office, but then he saw the name on the door: Tom Freston. But the man in the office was not the one Billy knew from his five years with the company.

"That's not Tom Freston. What the hell is going on here?"

"Sir, please come with us right now. Don't make us get physical."

Determined to uncover the truth, Billy allowed himself to be escorted out of the office building. The very fabric of his reality was unravelling, and Billy was going to piece it back together, no matter what.

For now, however, he was getting thrown out of the company he'd been loyally serving for the last five years to the likely detriment of his physical and mental well-being. He couldn't believe it. Part of him wanted to resist, even though he knew the security guards would easily subdue him. It didn't seem fair that this could happen. One day, he was with the company. The next, they were throwing him out on the street.

The guards went back inside once they'd escorted Billy off the premises, leaving him to stew in his angry, disbelieving thoughts. He just stared at the building, wondering what happened to turn his world upside-down. Then he felt a tap on his shoulder and whirled around to see the culprit.

"Hi Mr Stuart. A bit confused? Your day didn't start as normal, did it?"

Billy was surprised to see an attractive woman in front of him. She was in her early 30s and possessed an effortless allure. Her sun-kissed blonde hair cascaded down her shoulders in gentle waves. Her business pantsuit set was nothing short of impeccable; the tailored, charcoal grey blazer hugged her slender frame, accentuating her curves without being too revealing. Beneath the blazer, the woman wore a pristine white silk blouse that peeked out from a V-neck, lending a hint of sensuality to her attire. The fabric clung to her figure gracefully, emphasizing her slender neck and collarbones.

Her pants were equally stylish and refined, matching the shade of her blazer. They were tailored to perfection, flaring out slightly at the hips before seamlessly transitioning into a straight, elegant line. Her clothes flowed as she moved, exuding grace and poise. Completing the ensemble was a pair of sleek, high-heeled pumps that elongated her legs and added a touch of sophistication to her stride. Her accessories were minimal but tasteful: a delicate gold necklace adorned with a solitary, star-shaped diamond pendant and a matching pair of earrings.

Her makeup was subtle, accentuating her natural beauty rather than overpowering it. Her lips were painted with a soft, rosy shade, and her blue-green eyes were framed with mascara that made them sparkle with intelligence and charm. A faint, fresh scent lingered around her, some tasteful flowery perfume.

What struck Billy the most, however, was her smile. It could disarm anyone in an instant. *Who is she?* He thought. She seemed to know him, but he'd never met her before in his life. He'd remember if he had.

As if sensing his question, the woman handed Billy a business card, which read:

Ms Nancy Johnson

Special Transportation Liaison

Interdimensional Division

Galactic World Enterprises

2772 Main Street

Building 6, Floor 13, Room 44

Omaha, Nebraska, 68007

This would have seemed like a joke, if not for her inexplicable familiarity with Billy and his day-to-day. Her sudden appearance had stunned him into near-silence, but he couldn't resist the urge to seek answers.

"OK, Ms Johnson, how do you know my name, and most importantly, how do you know I'm not having my usual day?"

The woman, Ms Johnson, met his inquisitive gaze with a serene smile.

"If you'll allow me to explain," she said. With a graceful gesture, she pointed to a sleek black limousine waiting by the kerb. "Please get in, and I will answer all your questions."

With nothing to lose and his curiosity piqued, Billy took a leap of faith. He nodded in agreement and opened the door to the waiting limousine. As he settled into a plush leather seat, the mysterious woman followed suit. Without a word, the chauffeur closed the door, and the limo smoothly pulled away from the kerb, merging into the bustling traffic of the city.

Billy's heart raced with anticipation as he whipped his head around the limo and then pressed his face to the tinted windows to look at the passing cityscape. He stole a few glances at the enigmatic woman seated beside him, her poise and confidence undiminished by his frantic, frenzied movements. She spoke, her voice calm and composed.

"Mr Stuart, there has been a slight hitch in our efforts to comply with your request to..." She paused momentarily, as if carefully choosing her words. "To remove you from the office environment."

Billy's confusion deepened. "Remove me from the office environment? What on earth are you talking about?"

The woman leaned forward slightly; her eyes locked onto his.

"You see, Mr Stuart, you are a part of a select group of individuals who took advantage of a special 'sale promotion.' The promotion allows you to step away from the daily grind and the pressures of your job and go anywhere in time."

Billy gaped at her for what felt like minutes. He was practically exuding cynicism and disbelief, looking at her like she'd just suggested that they fly to Venus.

"And why would I want to do that? Why should I even believe you *can* do that? Who are you really, and what do you want from me?"

Ms Johnson smiled gently, a glint of sincerity in her eyes.

"I represent an organization that specializes in providing individuals like yourself with a fresh start, an opportunity to explore new horizons. We offer an escape from the monotony of being an office drone, a chance to rediscover your passions, a life that's free from the constraints of the 9-to-5 routine."

As the limousine glided through the city streets, Billy found himself torn between doubt and curiosity. He had always dreamed of breaking free from the corporate rat race, but this seemed too good to be true. Ms Johnson continued, her words as persuasive as her voice was titillating.

"Mr Stuart, we offered you a clean slate, a chance to embark on a new journey. But we could not uphold our end of the bargain. You paid for the service. You trusted us and we failed you. But we have a money-back guarantee if we do not do as you requested. All we ask is for you to trust us again, to try and succeed the second time where we could not the first. Will you consider our offer?"

Billy's mind raced with conflicting thoughts. He could not recall what he had asked this company to do for him. All he knew was that, apparently, he requested that he be removed from the office environment. Had his mind been wiped off all his memories? Or was this just the second part of this incredibly elaborate prank? He couldn't help but feel doubtful, but his scepticism had been worn down by Ms Johnson's beauty and persuasiveness. He couldn't deny that the allure of a life less ordinary beckoned to him; it had been beckoning for five years. Now that he had a chance to take it, he'd be a fool to pass it up. He took a deep breath before announcing his decision.

"Alright, Ms Johnson, I'm willing to listen. Tell me more about what I need to do." The woman flashed him her biggest smile yet, nodded, and launched into an explanation. She spoke slowly and carefully, as if well-aware that what she was saying sounded baffling to any ordinary person, and Billy took many minutes to turn it over in his mind before responding.

"So, you're saying that by reprogramming this interdimensional transmitter, you can send me back in time and space to where I originally requested?" He asked, trying to wrap his head around the concept.

"Exactly, Mr Stuart. We have corrected the initial technical error. You'll have the opportunity to reset your life, change your course, and explore new possibilities."

Billy took another deep breath, but his mind had already been made up.

"Alright, Ms Johnson. Let's do it. Take me back to where I originally requested. I'm ready for a fresh start."

Ms Johnson's smile widened, and she reached into her briefcase and retrieved a small, intricate device.

"Thank you, Mr Stuart. You won't regret this decision. Please trust me, and we'll have you on your way to a new beginning in no time."

Billy watched with a mixture of excitement and trepidation as Ms Johnson configured the mysterious device and placed it on his arm.

"Are you ready, sir?" She asked. Billy met Ms Johnson's gaze; his eyes were filled with determination.

"I'm ready," he replied, his voice steady despite the butterflies in his stomach. She nodded back at him, her expression reassuring.

"Remember, Mr Stuart, this is a rare opportunity. Embrace it with an open heart and an adventurous spirit. When you arrive at your chosen moment in time and space, the world will be your canvas."

With those words of encouragement, Ms Johnson activated the device. A soft azure glow enveloped Billy's wrist, casting an ethereal radiance across his face. Time seemed to stand still for a fleeting moment as he braced himself for what lay ahead. Then, he felt a strange sensation, as if he were being pulled in multiple dimensions at once. His surroundings dissolved into a whirlwind of colours and shapes, and he closed his eyes, surrendering to the swirling vortex. It didn't hurt, but it also didn't feel good. It was disorienting, even nauseating.

When Billy reopened his eyes, he found himself in an entirely different place, time, and position. The world around him was unfamiliar, and the possibilities stretched out before him like an open book. His nausea was gone, replaced with a weightlessness he hadn't felt in five years. He was unburdened by responsibilities and fatigue. He was more awake than he'd ever been, adrenaline coursing through his veins as he beheld a world upon which he could write his own story.

Then he heard a roar behind him, and he turned around.

A Saber-tooth tiger was approaching him. Just like that, the nausea returned. He was going to need all the adrenaline he could get.

Billy started running, but as he was a beleaguered office worker fleeing an apex predator, he didn't make it very far. His last thought at the Saber-tooth tiger pounced on him was *I guess the damn thing didn't work this time, either. No chance to get my money back now. What a worthless guarantee.*

The Invention of Dating

In a world of customs and old traditions that abound,

Where love and courtship wear a different gown,

A spark ignited our hearts.

Was it the invention of dating? That, I doubt.

No longer confined to the whims of fate, our two souls met
online to search our heart's state,

In different spaces we conversed, with a chance to laugh, to
talk, to share, to begin to know each other.

The freedom to explore love on one's own was a journey
where two strangers might connect,

Our destinies, our hearts, and where our souls intersect.

The first date, nervous laughter would fill the air but not in
our case, two strangers hoping for a love affair,

With bated breath and hopeful hearts aglow,

We step into Sydney's streets looking for a cozy hole to learn more of each other.

A dinner date, a movie, we had them all,

Conversations deep, and talks small, always felt like a gentle exchange, the subtle signs, the chemistry's embrace,

As we begin to find our special place.

The invention of dating, a modern art, we did not invent,

A canvas for emotions to impart, we did not invent,

A chance for love to blossom and ignite,

That we gave a chance to grow.

Through trials and errors, we learnt and grew, through laughter, tears, we held each other in a journey of discovery hand in hand, as we discussed finances, and the rest,

The promise of a love eternal we felt.

So, here's to the inventor of dating, because of it our hearts joined together and danced!

Because of this we had a chance for love to flourish and to thrive, creating a beautiful grand tapestry of us.

My Red!

When True Love Arrives

His preparations complete, Robert is all set to leave town tomorrow. Before he says goodbye, however, he stops by at his favourite bar.

As Robert walks through the familiar streets, he can't help but feel a pang of nostalgia. Robert packed everything he owned up in boxes, loaded up the truck and is ready for a new adventure in a different country. He's spent his entire life in Northport, NSW. Tomorrow, he'll leave it all behind.

Robert's favourite bar, *The White Sheep*, is a cozy place where he spent countless evenings with friends, sharing laughter, stories, and memories. Even his conversations with Sarah, the bartender, were quite exciting and fulfilling. It's only fitting that he stops by for one last drink before his departure.

As he enters the dimly lit bar, he smiles. The atmosphere feels just as warm and welcoming as always. Sarah, who's been pouring his drinks for years, greets him with an enormous smile and her familiar nod. He likes her nod; it makes her blonde hair sway back and forth over her face, partially hiding her features and making her look more mysterious. *I wonder if she does that for everyone, or just me*, Robert thinks to himself.

Robert takes a seat at the corner of the bar, where he's spent countless hours pondering life's mysteries. He orders his usual, a whiskey neat, and when it arrives, he sips it slowly, savouring the moment. A few regulars are scattered throughout the bar, engaged in hushed conversations while Sarah serves drinks and glances at him every so often. *The White Sheep* isn't as crowded as usual.

As the night wears on, Robert can't help but overhear a conversation at the adjacent table. A group of friends, all of whom he knows well, are reminiscing about their own experiences in the town. They talk about the late-night adventures, the festivals, and the sense of community that had always bound them together.

Listening to their heartfelt stories and laughter, Robert is suddenly overwhelmed by a sense of belonging that he had taken for granted. These people, this town, have been his home for so long. His decision to leave was driven by a new career opportunity; he wanted something new, something different. Now, he starts to wonder if he's making the right choice.

Robert soon finds himself engrossed in memories and the warmth of his hometown. The camaraderie, the familiarity, and the love he feels for the place and its people overtake him. He starts to doubt all the things that once made him want to leave. *Why now? Why this hesitation?* He thinks.

With a heavy heart, Robert realises that saying goodbye to this town, to the people who have been a part of his life for so long, is going to be harder than he had expected. His night at *The White Sheep* is planting a seed of doubt in his mind, making him wonder if there's more value in staying and continuing to build on the life he has here.

The bar slowly empties, and Robert remains deep in thought, torn between the allure of the unknown and the comfort of the familiar. He'd made the decision to leave impulsively, but he's come to realise that he needs to do more soul-searching before he can feel at peace with his departure—or his decision to stay. He can't say what he'd rather do.

Robert's heart skips a beat as Sarah, the bartender he's known for years, sits down next to him and takes his hand.

"Robert, I...your decision to leave has made me a little braver. I need to tell you something before you leave tomorrow, because I might not get another chance."

"What is it Sarah?" He asks. He looks into her eyes, and then down at her hand, holding his.

"Have you never wondered how I feel about you? How I hover over you when you come in? I mean, I can't blame you. It's not like I ever said anything to you before. But still. Didn't you ever think that meant something? That it wasn't just me doing my job?"

Her words hang in the air, and he can feel the weight of them sinking in. It doesn't feel oppressively heavy. It feels welcome, like something small and warm atop his chest. He looks into her eyes, which hold a depth of emotion he has never noticed before. The dimly lit bar suddenly feels like the most intimate place in the world.

"Sarah," he stammers, "I...I didn't realise. I mean, I've wondered sometimes, but I thought it was just you being nice. You've always been nice to me. I've always valued our friendship, but..."

Sarah gently squeezes his hand as he trails off. She continues, her voice trembling slightly.

"Robert, it's more than friendship for me. I've been in love with you for a long time. I didn't say anything because I didn't want to complicate your life, especially with your job and how you were always talking about going overseas. I didn't want to make that harder for you. I promised myself that I wouldn't. But now you're really about to go, and I can't keep this bottled up any longer."

The revelation takes Robert aback. He has always seen Sarah as a good friend, someone he can confide in and share stories with. He never expected this confession. His mind races as he tries to process the situation. He's spent so long planning for his departure, focusing on the new opportunities that await him in a different country. But now, he has to make a choice he never expected. He'd dreamed of traveling for years, but this is a dream he didn't know he'd had until this very moment.

His surroundings seem to fade into the background as Robert wrestles with his feelings and the sudden complexity of his decision. He knows that his choice will have a profound impact on both his and Sarah's lives.

As he looks into Sarah's eyes, he realises that leaving Northport means leaving behind not only the town and its people but also a chance at love and a future he had never considered. He can't possibly make this decision in an instant. He needs more time, even though he doubts there will ever be enough. He has to know, for certain, what his true feelings are and what he wants from his life.

"Sarah," he says after a lengthy pause, "I need some time to think about this. It's a lot to process, and I don't want to make a hasty decision. Can we talk more tomorrow?"

Sarah nods, her eyes glistening with tears. "Of course, Robert. Take all the time you need. Just know that whatever you decide, I'll support you. Now head home. I need to close up."

With that, Sarah releases his hand, wipes her eyes and retreats behind the counter. Robert returns to his thoughts, his heart torn between the adventure of leaving and the unexpected possibility of love that could last a lifetime. Soon, he finishes his drink, waving at Sarah as she cleans up. Looking at his watch, he notices the time: 2:30 AM. Time flew when he was with Sarah. He never noticed that before.

The next day, Robert meets with the real estate agent and hands him the keys to his home. He has lived there for many years, but he relinquishes it in a single moment.

It's 1 PM now. The bar will be open for the lunch hour rush, and Sarah will be there. He has to tell her about his decision.

Arriving at the bar, he notices a gloominess in the ambiance. Everyone is hushed, not engaging with each other as they normally do. They keep to themselves, heads down in their food and drinks. Sarah is nowhere to be found.

Robert takes his usual seat, scanning the lunch crowd for Sarah. The owner, Angus, comes over to him.

"The usual, Robert?"

"Yes, Angus, that will be great. By the way, do you know where Sarah is?"

Robert sees tears welling in Angus' eyes, and his heart sinks in his chest.

"You haven't heard? Sarah was killed in a head on collision last night on Remembrance Road near Picton. A drunken idiot swerved right in front of her. They both died instantly if that's any consolation. She wasn't in pain."

The two men remain there in silence, one standing and one sitting. Neither of them knows what to say. Robert's mind is a mess of thoughts, fighting against each other. Despair that she's gone. Disbelief that it ever could have happened. Anger at the nameless drunkard whose carelessness ended her life. Regret at letting her stew in her feelings for all these years and running away the night she confessed them. Maybe if he'd stayed and made his decision on the spot, she would still be alive. Now, he can't tell her. He never will.

"Let me get your drink," Angus says sombrely, trudging off behind the bar.

Angus returns with Robert's drink, sets it in front of him and with a nod leaves him to his thoughts.

In the time he was waiting, Robert made another decision. Without taking a sip, he gets up, throws a $20 note on the counter, and walks out of the bar. He gets in his truck and drives out of Northport. He never returns.

We Are Going to Write

Life in Northport, New South Wales, a small village south of Sydney, was idyllic as it could get. It had everything a small village should to ensure the comfort of its residents.

Main Street was covered in shops. The local bookshop, the barber, the hairdresser salon, a couple of pubs. Your butcher, baker and even a candle-stick maker of old had shops on Main Street.

Schoolchildren and adults alike frequented the library, which was located off Main Street on Hill Street. The library had clubs that would use its facilities. There were chess clubs, craft clubs, book clubs and one particular writer's group: Northport Writers.

The writer's group had been flourishing for years. Comprising a diverse array of talented older individuals, mostly retirees, it was a haven for creativity and support. However, every rose garden has its thorns, and in this case, those thorns were a group of mature women who acted quite immaturely. Despite being well past their teenage years, they drew ample inspiration from the movie *Mean Girls*.

Meet the Fabulous Four: Betty, the group's unofficial queen bee; Beatrice, the quiet but conniving one; Linda, who specialized in passive-aggressive comments; and Carol, a fashionista who was always quick to judge others based on their appearance. These women, although accomplished in their own right, had developed an odd clique that met for coffee before the writers group. They whispered and plotted like teenagers, made snide remarks, and conspired against their fellow writers.

Their target this year was Jonathan Pine, a nerdy, kind-hearted guy with a penchant for science fiction and wearing quirky t-shirts that proudly displayed his love for all things geeky. Jonathan was a prolific writer, creating fantastical worlds and intricate plots that captivated the imagination. However, his soft-spoken nature and unique style of writing made him an easy mark for the Fabulous Four.

One fateful Friday afternoon, the Fabulous Four decided it was time to put the devious plan they'd been stirring up for weeks into action. As Jonathan read aloud a brilliant excerpt from his latest science fiction novel, Betty whispered to Susan, "He's such a nerd. Does he even know how to dress like an adult?"

Linda, not to be outdone, leaned over, and added, "And have you seen his hair? It's like he's stuck in the '90s!"

Carol chimed in with a smirk on her face. "Maybe we should give him a makeover. You know, help him fit in with the rest of us."

Their whispers grew louder, and once he had finished his excerpt, they confronted Jonathan. With feigned kindness, they offered to take him shopping and help him choose some new, more 'mature' clothing.

Jonathan, eager to fit in and always open to self-improvement, accepted their offer, oblivious to their ulterior motives. He genuinely believed they were just being kind, offering friendship and mentorship.

Over the next few weeks, Jonathan wore button-down shirts and slacks that were entirely against his usual style. He was uncertain about his latest look but had faith that the Fabulous Four had his best interests at heart.

However, the changes weren't about his wardrobe. The women subtly undermined his writing, suggesting he 'tone down' his imaginative elements and write stories that were more 'realistic.' They claimed it was for his own good to appeal to a wider audience, but in reality, it was a subtle form of bullying.

As time passed, Jonathan grew increasingly unhappy. His writing lost its magic, and he felt like a shadow of his former self. Deep down, he knew something was wrong, but he couldn't articulate it. It wasn't in his nature to suspect others of wrongdoing and sabotage. It took a fellow writer, an outsider not in the group, to explain what was happening.

Emma, another local writer with whom Jonathan sometimes met and shared ideas, did not like the direction his recent writings were taking. She could tell that someone was warping his creative voice and vision, forcing him to write outside his preferred genre and emulate a style with which he was unfamiliar. All of the 'Jonathan' had gone out of his works.

After some prying, she learned that four older women in the writer's group had been mentoring him. Suspicious of their methods and their movies, Emma joined the writer's group to see for herself the actions of the Fabulous Four.

One day, Emma took Jonathan aside. She gently but firmly pointed out the changes in him and the behaviour of the Fabulous Four. She encouraged him to stay true to his unique voice and style, reassuring him that he didn't need to change for anyone.

Jonathan, finally realizing the truth, thanked Emma for her support. With newfound confidence, he decided he should confront the Fabulous Four. But first, he was going to take their advice. Though they didn't realise it, they had given him inspiration after all.

Jonathan missed the rest of the year's writer's group meetings. The Fabulous Four were confident they had gotten ridded of the odd ball for good.

After Christmas, however, the group met for the first meeting of the year, and Jonathan strolled in. He was dressed in one of his quirky t-shirts and was holding a box. He asked if he could speak to the group. The group president, who was happy to see him again, nodded his approval.

"Members of the Northport Writers, I want to apologise to you for not attending the last months of our writing sessions. But I had good reason, which I would love to share with you today."

Jonathan reached into the box and took out many books, which he laid on the table. When he was done, there were over 25 copies. Johnathan picked one up and turned the book towards the members so they could see the front cover.

"Dear members. This is my newly published novel, which was taken up by Blueprint press and has been the number one bestseller in the Sydney Times for seven weeks running."

Several members give out gasps and whoops of joy for Jonathan, and many clapped their approval.

The Fabulous Four just stared at him, their eyes wide in disbelief.

"I wanted to share these accomplishments with the four members of this group who inspired the novel. Betty, Beatrice, Linda, and Carol, you four ladies were my muses. Without you, I never would have written this novel, which I received notice today will be made into a TV series for the 2025 season by Channel 7."

The Fabulous Four's mood changed. As they listened to Jonathan, a tenderness, of sorts, entered their hearts. They had set out to torment him and stifle his creativity, but instead had inspired him. They only briefly considered their ill intent, as Linda leaned to Betty and remarked: "Maybe we shouldn't have been so mean."

But mainly, they were just excited to have been the inspiration for a famous novel. They thought that, perhaps, Jonathan would credit them in interviews or even in the book itself, leading to their own renown. The Fabulous Four, though touched by his kindness, were already anticipating how this could benefit them.

"Now, without further ado, I want to present each member of this writer's group with a signed copy of my recent novel, titled *The Witches of Northport*."

Laughter erupted throughout the room as everyone realised Jonathan's inspiration. He had modelled the witches after the Fabulous Four!

"This is insulting," cried out Betty.

"I cannot believe you did this!" Exclaimed Linda.

"How could you, Jonathan?" snapped Carol, nearly on the brink of tears.

"So not tight," was all that Beatrice could muster.

The Fabulous Four got up from their chairs and headed towards the door. On her way out, Betty turned around and declared: "We quit this group!" Then she stormed out for good, followed by the other three women.

Jonathan's courage took back the Fabulous Four; he called them out for their mean-spirited antics that before had been just barely tolerated. The rest of the group rallied behind him, and the toxic clique soon dissolved.

Jonathan continued to write with renewed passion, his imagination soaring once more. The Northport writer's group became a more inclusive and supportive community, with each member embracing their unique talents and quirks, free from the toxic influence of the Fabulous Four.

And in a fitting twist of fate, the local media, national media and even the international media were hungry for interviews with the Fabulous Four. Paparazzi, for all the wrong reasons, chased after them for photos. Their 'mentorship' had backfired, catapulting them to infamy rather than fame. Now, they preferred to hide rather than stand out.

Meanwhile, every time Jonathan walked into the writer's group meeting, all he could think of was the line from *Mean Girls* but amended: *Get out losers. We are going to write.*

Change

The grand chandelier in the opulent ballroom cast a warm, inviting glow over the elegant guests gathered at the extravagant gala. Michael, the host of the evening, moved through the crowd with a charismatic smile, introducing friends and acquaintances to one another. As the night went on, he couldn't help but notice the intriguing dynamics of the people he had brought together.

One particular introduction stood out that evening. Michael brought Larry, a tall and charming man, over to meet Mary, a graceful and vivacious woman. He leaned in close to Larry and whispered, "Larry, I'd like you to meet Mary. She's new to the city, and I think you two would hit it off."

Larry extended his hand, an easy grin on his face, and said, "It's a pleasure to meet you, Mary."

Mary, her eyes sparkling with interest, took Larry's hand and replied, "Likewise, Larry. I've been looking forward to meeting new people."

The moment their hands touched; an unspoken recognition flickered between them. Both their eyes widened imperceptibly. Larry and Mary had a history that ran deeper than this casual introduction. They had met before, under somewhat awkward circumstances.

Larry was a homicide detective and Mary was a 'lady of the night.' Their paths crossed one night when Larry was called to the scene of a crime.

Upon arriving, Larry found a man lying on a bed, covered in blood. Standing near the corpse was Mary, blood smeared all over her half-naked body. She wore nothing save for a bedsheet that was wrapped around her waist.

Splatter or something else, thought Larry as he went up to the first officers to arrive on the scene. He spent a few minutes talking with them to get all the details. Once they told him everything they knew, he approached Mary. She was remarkably cogent for the suspect of a brutal murder, and with her testimony, as well as forensic evidence and camera footage, they found the real culprit: the victim's wife.

Mary was not involved any more with the police after that, but she kept Larry's card and called him a few months afterwards asking for a quick meeting over coffee. Though surprised that she contacted him out of the blue, Larry accepted.

Life has a funny way of connecting individuals. This meeting, between a detective and one of his witnesses, led to the development of their close friendship. They became confidants and even had a short-lived romance that neither of them would ever forget. Yet, for reasons known only to them, they had drifted apart, and their paths hadn't crossed for several years.

Michael, unaware of the prior history between the two, soon excused himself to attend to other guests. Left alone in the party's swirl, Larry and Mary stood in awkward silence. They exchanged nervous glances, both unsure of how to proceed.

After what felt like an eternity, Larry finally spoke, his voice filled with a mix of surprise and amusement.

"Mary, it's been ages. I never expected to see you here."

Mary chuckled softly; her eyes locked onto Larry's.

"Yes, it has been a long time, Larry. You look great."

Larry's smile grew warmer, and he replied, "While you're even more beautiful than I remember."

"Are you still in homicide?" Asked Mary.

"I am. How about you Mary? What have you been up to?"

Mary did not answer, and Larry did not press the issue, but he suspected the truth. Mary's occupation hadn't changed since their first meeting. This awkwardness aside, their banter was easy, and the years melted away as they reminisced about the good times they had shared. They laughed about their inside jokes, the places they used to visit, and the countless memories they had made together. It was as if no time had passed at all.

As the conversation flowed, they gradually rejoined the party, chatting and laughing as if they had never lost touch. The chemistry between them was undeniable, and those around them couldn't help but notice their connection.

The night continued, and the gala was a tremendous success. For Larry and Mary, the highlight was undoubtedly their unexpected reunion. They didn't need words to acknowledge the past; their renewed friendship was enough to fill the void created by their years apart.

When the gala ended and Michael once again found them chatting together, he remarked with a knowing smile, "I see you two have hit it off. I knew you would."

Larry and Mary exchanged a glance, their secret history still unspoken but deeply understood by both. With a shared smile and a nod, they both bid Michael a good evening. Before they could leave, however, their host took Larry by the arm.

"Wait, Larry. A quick word before you leave." Mary took this opportunity to depart, and they both watched as she grabbed her coat and made an elegant exit.

"Well buddy, did you hit it off? It sure looked that way to me."

"We did. I appreciate the introduction, but while we had a great time, I don't think we'll be taking our acquaintance any further than tonight."

"Why? You both looked so smart together. You were like two puzzle pieces out there, the perfect fit. I'm sure I'm not the only one who noticed."

"That might be the impression, but sometimes not everything is what it seems."

"What do you mean?" Micheal asked. Larry just sighed and laid a hand on his shoulder.

"Drop it, Michael. It won't happen. Thanks for the evening. It was...different."

Larry shook his bewildered host's hand and strode out the front door.

As Larry walked to his car, he considered what Michael had said. They did go well together; they always had. But no one besides Larry and Mary themselves knew why they would never work out. They were both keenly aware of the reason; it was an unspoken agreement between them, a topic they knew was best left untouched.

They both loved their jobs and would not ask the other to change.

What's For Dinner

Deep within the heart of a sprawling, ancient forest, Sally, and Jill found themselves hopelessly lost. They had ventured too far from home, their curiosity leading them further and further away, until the dense canopy of trees had swallowed them whole. Worse yet, they weren't alone. With them was their little sister, Nancy, who clung to Jill for comfort as tears welled up in her eyes.

As the sun dipped below the horizon, casting long shadows, and painting the woods in eerie twilight, the siblings stumbled upon a clearing unlike any they'd ever seen. A gnarled oak tree loomed in the center, its branches clawing at the sky like skeletal fingers. At the base of the tree sat a woman, her face hidden beneath a hood. Her presence was unsettling, as if there was some stifling aura around her that incited agitation.

Sally and Jill exchanged worried glances. They'd heard tales of witches and sorceresses who roamed these woods. Now, this figure appeared before them, and she looked like something straight out of those old stories.

The witch spoke, her voice an unnerving whisper carried by the wind. "Ah, lost souls," she crooned, her eyes glinting with an otherworldly light. "I can offer you everything you've ever desired—wealth, power, and happiness. But in exchange, I require your precious baby sister."

Nancy whimpered in Jill's arms, clutching her sister's shirt tighter. The older sisters' hearts ached at the thought of giving up their beloved sibling. They knew they couldn't trust this mysterious figure.

"We need a moment to discuss your offer," Sally said, her voice trembling.

The witch nodded, her eyes never leaving Nancy. As the witch waited, Sally and Jill huddled together, their minds racing almost as fast as their hearts.

"We can't give up, Nancy," Jill whispered urgently. "But we can't just refuse her outright, either. She's clearly powerful."

Sally nodded. "We need a plan, some way to defend ourselves while we escape with Nancy."

As they spoke, Sally noticed a glint of metal near the witch's feet—a small, ancient-looking dagger half-hidden in the underbrush. She saw a chance they couldn't pass up.

"We'll agree to her offer, temporarily," Sally whispered. "Then, when she's distracted, I'll grab that dagger and we'll make a run for it."

With heavy hearts bent towards the grim plan they were about to undertake, they turned back to the witch.

"We accept your offer," Sally announced, trying to keep her voice steady.

The witch smiled wickedly, exposing rows of crooked, yellowing teeth as she extended her hand towards Nancy. But just as she did, a sudden rustling in the bushes behind her caught her attention. Sally had seized the dagger.

With lightning speed, Sally dashed into the forest with Jill holding Nancy in tow, their footsteps muffled by the fallen leaves. The witch, disoriented and furious, gave chase, but the sisters used their knowledge of the woods to their advantage and disappeared among the trees and shadows.

They ran for hours, adrenaline fuelling their escape. Finally, as the first rays of dawn broke through the trees, they stumbled upon a familiar path that led them back to their village. They both breathed out sighs of relief, and Jill held her baby sister tight in her arms. Nancy, too, seemed to calm down at the familiar sight of home. Sally's grip on the dagger loosened as she embraced Jill with her free hand.

"We did it. We really did it," she murmured, near tears. Jill hugged her back, setting Nancy down, and the two of them pulled their younger sister into the embrace. Once they calmed their spirits, adjusting to the fact that they were safe once again, they walked back to their family's house. They moved slowly, as little Nancy was now walking on her own two feet. They came to the comforting sight of their front door, and Sally pushed it open.

Sally and Jill froze in the doorway, their hearts pounding once again with a mixture of fear and confusion. The sight before them was almost surreal. There, in their own cozy home, the witch was sitting at the kitchen table, sipping tea with their parents. Their mother, who had been standing, turned to them with a warm but unsettling smile.

"We just made a deal with this witch," she said, her tone calm and matter-of-fact. "Nancy, come here."

Nancy hesitated for a moment before taking a few tentative steps towards her mother. The witch's presence seemed to have a strange effect on their parents, making them oddly compliant.

Sally and Jill maintained their composure, though internally they were panicking. They needed to figure out what was happening and how to protect their sister.

"What kind of deal did you make?" Sally asked, her eyes darting between her parents and the witch. The witch, who had an air of smug satisfaction about her, gently set her teacup down.

"Oh, a simple one, no different from the deal you could have made," she replied with a toothy grin. "Your parents wanted wealth and power, and in exchange, they offered me dear Nancy."

Jill couldn't help but speak up, her voice trembling with anger and fear. Her composure was gone; this was too horrible to let stand.

"How could you make such a deal without our consent? Nancy is our sister, your daughter! This woman has no right to take her!"

Their mother, still smiling unnaturally, replied, "We thought it was for the best, dear. You two will have a much brighter future this way." Their father nodded absentmindedly along with his wife's words.

Sally and Jill realised that the witch's presence had somehow clouded their parents' judgment and diminished their free will. They would never be acting like this otherwise. They needed a plan, and fast. Thinking on her feet, Sally subtly gestured for Jill to follow her back outside. Once out of sight and earshot of their parents and the witch, they spoke in hushed tones.

"Our parents are under her influence. We have to break that spell somehow," Sally whispered urgently.

Jill nodded in agreement, her mind racing for a solution.

"We need to find something that can counteract her magic. Maybe there's a way to break her hold over them." They didn't have a better plan, not yet, so Sally nodded and stepped back inside.

"Mother, Jill, and I need to discuss this proposition. We need a minute," she said.

"Of course, dear. Take your time."

The sisters went into the lounge to draw up a plan, but as much as they tried, a solution eluded them. They had no clue where this witch's magic came from, or how to counteract it. If they tried to wrest Nancy from their parents with brute force, they would almost certainly be stopped. They couldn't reason with them, not while they were under the witch's sway. All hope seemed lost.

Then, as if to confirm their fears, they heard a bloodcurdling shriek and a series of thuds. Sally's heart sank as she realised she didn't have the dagger with her. The sisters rushed back into the kitchen, terrified that the witch had gotten tired of waiting.

A horrifying scene greeted them. The witch lay sprawled on the floor, the dagger plunged into her chest. Nancy's trembling hands were stained with blood. As disturbing as it was, they were at least relieved to see that it wasn't Nancy who'd been killed.

"Nancy, what have you done?" Jill gasped, rushing over to her baby sister, who looked both terrified and relieved.

Their mother, no longer wearing her eerie smile, explained, "Nancy broke the enchantment over us. She acted on her own to protect herself and us."

Sally knelt beside Nancy, her voice trembling with a mixture of awe and fear as she spoke.

"How did you do it, Nancy?"

Nancy, tears streaming down her face, whispered, "The witch wanted to take me away, and I didn't want to leave you both. So, I...I took the dagger from you when you weren't looking, and I hurt the witch with it...I'm sorry."

Their father gently placed a hand on Nancy's shoulder.

"You did what you had to do, sweetheart. The witch's magic blinded us, but you broke the spell. You're our hero."

Sally and Jill hugged their sister tightly, overwhelmed with a mix of emotions. They knew that Nancy's actions had saved them all from a sinister fate. The witch was no longer a menace. But they were also unsettled by the brutal act of violence that their sister had committed. She was no more than a child, and yet she was covered in blood.

As they comforted Nancy, they saw the witch's body slowly crumble into ash, leaving behind only the dagger, now cleansed of dark magic. Nancy broke from their embrace and walked over to the blade. She picked it off the ground, turned it over in her hands and said: "Mother, I'm hungry. What's for dinner?"

Marriage is in the Cards

The day had finally come, the day that humanity had spent generations preparing for. Earth's sun, once a brilliant beacon of life, was now flickering like a dying candle, and its light was growing dim. Scientists had long warned this event, and their words of caution had spurred humanity to act.

When scientists predicted the death of Earth's sun in 2024, it was a call to action for all the world. Great minds from every country came together to develop a contingency plan. They constructed enormous building-sized lights, like towering lighthouses in the sky, over each major city on Earth. These colossal structures, powered by advanced technology, replaced the waning sun's light and warmth, ensuring that life on the planet could continue even as its original source of light faded.

As the day drew nearer, people from every corner of the world watched in awe and anticipation as beams of light descended from the artificial suns in the sky. These beams, synchronized precisely, were supposed to spread like a banket over the world. However, for some unknown reason, they all pointed towards an ordinary man named William Robert Johnson, or Billy Bob to his friends and neighbours.

Billy Bob was a humble farmer who loved to play card games and lived in Australia in the small, quiet village of Northport, New South Wales. 85 kilometres north of Northport, one of the artificial suns had been erected over the bustling city of Sydney. It, like all the others, directed its light at the bemused farmer.

At first, the beams that converged upon him puzzled the residents of Billy Bob's village. As the world outside grew darker with each passing day, the villagers wondered about Billy Bob, their small village, the cities around the world, and if they had indeed executed the right plan. But as days turned into weeks, the villagers realised that the beams of light had a purpose, and that purpose revolved around Billy Bob Johnson.

The attention he was suddenly receiving baffled Billy Bob, a simple and unassuming man. He had no unique skills or knowledge, and he could not fathom why he had become the focal point of the beams of light that were supposed to brighten the planet. Every evening, he would walk out into his fields, gaze up at the heavens and watch the beams of light that pointed down at him with their unyielding intensity.

The scientific community and world leaders, meanwhile, were in a race against time. They knew that the artificial lights would not be enough to sustain life on Earth indefinitely. They had been buying time, but they needed to find a more permanent solution, a new star, or a way to rekindle the dying sun. It was a monumental challenge that taxed the collective intelligence and resources of humanity.

As the months passed, Billy Bob's purpose became clearer. He felt different, and he shared this with the many scientists who studied him and conducted experiments, all to determine why the beams focused on Billy Bob.

Not one experiment or test told the scientists anything.

Amid this turmoil, Billy Bob remained a humble farmer, struggling to understand what he was feeling. He took solace in his cards, occupying himself as the world seemed to increasingly revolve around him. It was one day when he was by himself, playing a game of solitaire, that he received a strange message in his mind that illuminated his purpose.

"You, William Robert Johnson, are the one we have chosen!"

The thought entered Billy Bob's mind out of nowhere. At first, he didn't realise it belonged to someone else.

"Must be daydreaming," he muttered aloud as he looked up from his cards. He got up and started walking around, hoping to jar his mind into alertness. Then, the voice came back.

"You are not dreaming, William Robert Johnson. This is Central Control communicating with you."

"What the heck is Central Control?" Now, Billy Bob was starting to realise that these weren't his own thoughts. He didn't know what else to do other than respond.

"We are communicating to you about the future. It is the year 3424, and we need to tell you that these building-sized lights will not help Earth but destroy it. The solution lies in you."

"In me? What do you mean by that? The lights are supposed to save us. Everyone says the world's gonna end without them."

"We have diverted the beams to shine on you so that scientists can study you and find the answer."

"The scientists have done all kinds of tests and experiments. They haven't found anything. Please let me alone."

"No, William Robert Johnson, we will not leave you alone. You must tell the scientists that they have not looked deep enough in you."

"Deep in me? What do you mean?"

"Your DNA. Tell them the answer is in your DNA. This is our last transmission. We have no more power left. Good luck. The future of humanity rests on your shoulders."

With that parting message, the beams of light stopped transmitting from the building-sized lights and darkness again prevailed over all of Northport.

Billy Bob felt a sense of bewilderment. What had happened? Part of him was still convinced that all this must have been a dream, but he knew it couldn't be. After all, the voice said they had lost all power, and the lights shut off immediately after. It couldn't possibly be a coincidence.

"It has to be real," he murmured to himself. He could think of no other explanation. And if it was real, he did indeed have a role to play. He didn't understand it, but he had his orders. In the morning, he called up the lead scientist and told her to run a DNA test on him. She was sceptical at first, but eventually Dr Amelia Peterson decided that it couldn't hurt. She scheduled the test for him.

Following Billy Bob's DNA test, the scientific community made an incredible breakthrough. They found a unique genetic marker within Billy Bob's DNA that held the secret to creating an alternative energy source, one that might rejuvenate the dying sun. The world watched anxiously as scientists worked tirelessly to develop a solution.

Months turned into years, and the day finally came when humanity's plan succeeded. Using the knowledge they gleaned from Billy Bob's genetic marker, they reignited the sun, restoring its brilliant light and warmth. The artificial lights in the sky slowly dimmed, their mission complete.

Billy Bob Johnson, who had unwittingly become a symbol of hope for humanity, returned to his simple life as a farmer. He continued his work around the farm and played his card games, never understanding the magnitude of his role in saving the world. He was just content to have played a part in this incredible journey, ensuring the survival of the people and the planet he loved.

As the Earth bathed in the renewed warmth of its sun, the planet thrived once more. Billy Bob Johnson became a legend, though you'd never know it by talking to him. He was ego-less, completely unaltered by his status as Earth's saviour. So, he went about his life as if nothing had ever happened until one day he received another telepathic message.

"Well done. You have saved humankind not only in your timeline but in ours."

Recognising the voice, Billy Bob thought his answer: "Oh, it was nothing. I just did what you said to do. Thank you for that, by the way. Though I feel a bit rude; I never did get your name. Who am I speaking to?"

For several moments, the telepathic communication stopped. Billy Bob wondered if whatever was allowing them to talk had been disconnected, but then he received an answer: "My name is William Robert Johnson XXV."

Billy Bob was stunned. "Are we related?"

"Yes Sir. You are my ancestor."

"But I'm not even married. How is this possible?"

Then, there was a knock on the door.

"Excuse me, someone's at the door," he thought to the voice in his head. Billy Bob went to answer it, and upon opening the door, he saw one of the most beautiful women he had ever met.

"Mr Johnson, my name is Regina Frankston. I just joined Dr Amelia Peterson's team and I'm here for some follow up. May I come in?"

The voice in Billy Bob's mind said: "You soon will be."

Until Death Do Us Apart

In the year 3024, Australia had undergone a radical transformation. The vast continent had become one sprawling metropolis, stretching from the east coast to the west, from the north to the south. The Australian Outback, once a symbol of rugged wilderness, had become a distant memory, buried beneath layers of concrete and steel.

In the heart of this colossal city, the remnants of natural beauty could only be found within a small, mysterious area at the geographical center of the continent. This region was considered uninhabitable by most, a barren and desolate expanse that few dared to venture into. However, it was precisely here that an extraordinary community of beings had taken root: the Venusians.

The Venusians were refugees from the planet Venus. Their home planet had become increasingly inhospitable due to climate change, so they had embarked on a daring interplanetary journey to Earth, seeking refuge. It was a journey fraught with peril, but their advanced technology allowed them to survive the treacherous voyage.

Upon arriving in Australia, they found the heart of the continent strangely reminiscent of the harsh conditions they had faced on Venus. This unique similarity drew them in, and after negotiating a fantastic treaty between Australia and the rest of the world, they settled in this desolate region. Over time, they manipulated the unforgiving environment and developed a sustainable way of life.

The Venusians lived in vast underground cities, their architecture blending seamlessly with the natural rock formations of the region. They had mastered the art of harnessing geothermal energy to provide power to their homes and regulate the temperature of their resorts.

The Venusians' sophisticated hydroponic systems allowed them to grow food in the otherwise barren land. Their air filtration systems extracted precious oxygen from the thin atmosphere, ensuring their survival. They were a resilient and resourceful people who had learned to appreciate the stark beauty of their surroundings, finding solace in the vast crimson plains and the otherworldly rock formations that dotted the landscape. Their culture had evolved to embrace simplicity, sustainability, and a deep connection to the natural world.

They had also established a unique relationship with the surviving native wildlife. The Venusians coexisted with the local fauna, forming a delicate balance in their shared ecosystem.

Despite their relative isolation, the Venusians were not entirely cut off from the rest of the world. They maintained contact with Australia's mega-city, exchanging knowledge and resources when necessary. Their resorts were also frequented by tourists from all over the world since they were quite a novelty.

However, the Venusians were determined to protect their way of life and the fragile environment they cherished.

As time passed, stories of the Venusians living in the heart of Australia became the stuff of legend. Their existence served as a reminder that even in the most extreme and inhospitable conditions, life could not only survive but thrive. They had found a new home on Earth, and in doing so, had breathed life into a lifeless land, forging a connection between two worlds that spanned the vastness of space and time.

This was what Amelia Kelly read when she checked out the travel brochures featuring the 'Inferno Outback,' a harsh and barren land where the sun beat down mercilessly, and the ground scorched everything that touched it.

Amelia read that few ventured there, and those who did often returned with tales of unforgiving heat, unyielding terrain, and sheer excitement. But Amelia Kelly wanted to see it, and, after much cajoling of her husband Angus, they set out by themselves to see the remarkable community that had made a home in the oppressive conditions of the Outback.

Angus and Amelia had been married 28 years, and while the first few years had been good for Amelia, for the rest of their marriage she felt as if she'd been living in a hellish environment, much like the Inferno Outback itself.

Until death do us part, Amelia thought bitterly.

Departing from Yorkers Pine Beach in what used to be northern Queensland, Angus and Amelia packed up their hovercraft with all the essentials for their trek, hoping they had all the right supplies to tackle the Inferno Outback.

Amelia had looked up directions, and getting there was relatively easy. Taking AU 178 (what used to be called the A6), the couple headed west and stopped at Julia Creek for a coffee and a short rest. After an hour, they got back into their hovercraft and continued until reaching AU 332 just south of Costello, what was known as the Northern Territory in olden times.

Amelia's cousin Matilda lived in Simpson with her partner and two children, and the two hadn't seen each other in a long time. Amelia had long wanted to get together, and this trip provided the perfect opportunity. So, on their way to the Infernal Outback, she and Angus stopped at Matilda's house. They enjoyed a hardy lunch and some excellent wine from the old mining caves of Simpson.

Angus never liked Matilda, but the extra driving was worth it to keep his wife from complaining.

After they finished their lunch, Angus pointed the hovercraft towards the dried-up mines in Coober Pedy in the old geographical area once known as South Australia, now referred to as SA Section 45. From here on out, it was easy coasting. Amelia relieved Angus of the controls and steered them towards AU 234, straight into the Inferno Outback.

Amelia started to slow the hovercraft when she saw Mead, the Venusians' massive dome city, looming in the distance. Mead encompassed the entirety of what was once called the Great Victoria Desert. It was far smaller than the dome that had been built over Australia, but at 422,466 square kilometres, It could clearly be seen from outer space. Amelia read in *Scientific World* magazine that astronaut Miriam Vassallo had described Mead as "a bubble inside a bubble."

The Venusians had chosen to settle in the desert for its arid conditions, and once they built the dome, they were able to control the climate within it, making it even hotter. Humans needed to wear special coolant suits to survive within Mead. Even then, the suits would only protect them for 4 hours. Those who remained in the city after the coolant was depleted would die in ten minutes. Fortunately for the tourists, and Mead's tourism industry, there were various human-oriented resorts on the outskirts of the city where people could replenish their coolant supply.

Amelia pulled the hovercraft in at the control entry point, and she and Angus showed their ID chips. The AI in charge of the entry point scanned their chips and let them through, pointing them to the Adivar Resort, where they had reservations.

Checking into the 10-star resort was a delight. The AI concierge recognised them upon their arrival and took their bags to their room and remotely drove their hovercraft to their parking space. As they were being led to their room, the concierge took a few minutes to show them the best parts of the resort. Amelia was delighted by the pool, while even grumpy Angus couldn't help but grin when he saw the size of the bar. As the tour didn't take long, they soon arrived on floor 65, where they would be staying.

The concierge left the couple to their own devices once they reached the room. Amelia flopped down on the bed, letting out a deep sigh as she relaxed atop the soft covers and plush mattress, while Angus got started whining right away.

"Six hours of driving, and one spent having to stomach your cousin, her brats, and that boring husband of hers. I swear, trying to hold a conversation with the man is like pulling teeth! I never liked them and never will."

"Angus, sweetheart, don't fret. Our vacation's only going to get better from here. Tonight, I made reservations for dinner at the *Emperor* on level 40. It's a fusion restaurant that combines traditional Chinese cuisine and Venusian underground delicacies. Then, early tomorrow, we're going on a tour of the desert. Won't that be fun?."

"You can call it fun all you want; I call a waste of credits and time. I don't understand why you thought I'd like this. You know I hate anything Venusian."

"Sweetie, this will give you an opportunity to get to learn more about their culture and their people. I'm sure you'll be singing a different tune when we meet a real-life Venusian in the desert!"

Angus just grunted dismissively.

"Whatever. I'm going to take a shower before dinner, and then it's straight to bed. I'm exhausted. What time are we heading out?"

"5 AM, sweetie."

"Damn Amelia, only you would pick a time like that. Why can't we go out later, like normal people?"

"At 5 in the morning, you can see the first rays of the sun coming up on the desert. They say it's one of the most beautiful sights in the world."

"Yes, beautiful," Angus scoffed. "You know what else they say? That those early morning rays are the hottest of the day. You're crazy to want to go out in that heat."

"We'll be fine, sweetie; we'll have our coolant suits. Just you wait; you'll have the experience of a lifetime. I promise."

With nothing more than a noncommittal grunt, Angus lumbered off towards the shower, leaving Amelia with her thoughts. She watched him with a big grin on her face.

Oh yes, Angus. The experience of a lifetime.

Dinner, as always, was a hassle. Angus loudly announced that he hated everything on the menu without even reading it. Amelia tried pleading, coaxing, and coddling him as if he was a child, but she couldn't get him to pick something. He would not budge.

"I'm a chicken schnitzel and mash and no veggies type of guy. After 28 years of marriage, you should know that. Stop trying to get me to sample all this weird food."

So, in the middle of the *Emperor*, loud enough for all to hear, Angus ordered a chicken schnitzel and mash and no veggies with mushroom gravy. The other diners looked around, bemused, and mildly annoyed by the commotion. Judging from the look of disgust on the holographic server's face, Amelia was convinced that AI did, in fact, feel emotion.

After the tense dinner was over, the couple retired to their room to prepare for their early day. Angus never liked to rush, so last night Amelia said she would set their alarm go at 4 AM, giving him time to dress and get ready. He complained about that, too.

At 4 AM, the alarm sounded. Both Angus and Amelia went through their morning routine and were ready to leave the resort at 5 AM sharp. They took the hover shuttle and arrived at the point of departure at exactly 5:03. There, a holographic tour guide greeted them and instructed them on how to don their pressure suits and monitor their coolant levels. Both Amelia and Angus paid close attention to the instructions on the mechanics of the suit.

"Remember," said the guide, "you have 4 hours of coolant, so I recommend you spend no more than 3 hours out in the desert. For an optimal experience, you can take half that time to explore and half that time coming back, leaving one hour of coolant just in case you stop and see the sights for longer than you anticipated. We find that newcomers to Mead can lose track of time taking in all the city's wonders and conversing with the local Venusians. And please keep in mind that once you step out, you cannot communicate with the resort. No audio or video. You will be roughing it, just like in the old days. Now let me start your coolant."

"Wait one minute, you're not coming with us?" Angus blurted out in disbelief.

"No sir. Holograms cannot survive the atmosphere out in the Inferno Outback, but do not worry; you have the best equipment to do this self-guided tour."

"Damn it, Amelia. Did you know this?"

"Yes, I did, sweetie, but it's totally safe, I promise. I did my research."

Once their suits were set up, the holographic guide asked: "Are you ready?"

Angus was visibly fuming but, having nothing better to do, nodded along with Amelia—who looked far more excited—and steeled himself to exit the safety of the resort and head out into the Inferno Outback.

"I can't wait to meet a Venusian!" Amelia exclaimed. She had read that they were easy to spot in their underground cities.

"Standing in the sweltering heat talking to some alien. What a great way to spend a vacation," Angus muttered to himself.

The couple then proceeded to walk through the vacuum-sealed double doors at the edge of the resort. The first door closed behind them as they stepped through, and after a few moments of allowing the outdoor heat to filter into the area, the second door opened to reveal the Inferno Outback sprawling into the distance before them.

"Damn, even with the coolant suits, I feel the heat. Amelia, is this a good idea?"

"Yes Angus. This is a great idea. Don't you worry; I planned for everything."

Amelia encouraged Angus to go out first, and after several minutes of bickering, he acquiesced. As he tentatively stepped across the threshold of the resort and the desert, Amelia took a small pin in her suit pocket and punctured two small holes in his coolant delivery system without Angus being any the wiser.

"Come on, sweetie. Let's find the Venusians."

Angus looked at his watch.

"OK, just walking through the vacuum chamber to get outside took seven minutes. I'll watch our time and your coolant supply. You watch mine, OK?"

"Of course, sweetie. Check my coolant supply now."

Angus went behind Amelia and looked at her meter. She had 233 minutes.

"Amelia, you have 233 minutes. How much do I have?"

Amelia looked at the meter on the back of her husband's suit; it showed 206 minutes. *Good,* Amelia thought to herself, *it's escaping faster than I calculated.*

"The same, sweetie," she lied.

"Good. Alright, let's get this damn self-guided tour over with."

After walking for a while, Amelia asked Angus to check her coolant level, and after he did so, she checked his. Amelia reported to Angus that his was the same as hers, and they kept walking.

Amelia enjoyed seeing the vast expanse of Mead, but her enjoyment of the tour was hampered by her anticipation of what was to come. Angus was even less engaged; he kept complaining about the heat, looking at his watch incessantly, and asking Amelia to check his coolant levels. To make matters worse, neither of them saw a single "damn Venusian," as Angus called them.

Angus looked at his watch for what Amelia conservatively estimated to be the thousandth time and announced: "We've gone over the 1½ hour limit the hologram recommended. Time to head back, Amelia. Let me check your coolant level."

Amelia stood still, letting her husband read the meter on her back. She pulled out her pin, holding it carefully, so it stayed out of sight without piercing her suit.

"You have 142 minutes left. Plenty of time. How about me?"

When Amelia went behind Angus to check, she pricked a few more holes in the coolant system. His levels were already depleting rapidly, but she saw no reason not to expedite the process.

"The same sweetie. We're OK. Let's head back."

As they walked back, Amelia made sure they stopped to see some of the cherry-coloured plains and odd rock formations, much to Angus' chagrin.

"Come on, Amelia," snapped Angus, looking at his watch. "We're down to just 70 minutes; I'm not spending any more time out here than I have to."

"Of course, sweetie. I'm coming."

As the two set off again, Angus yelped as a loud beep came from his suit. Then, it announced: "Danger. You have reached the last of your coolant. You have 10 minutes to reach the resort. Danger. You must act now."

In a panic, Angus whirled around looked at Amelia.

"Damn, I've run out! You said I had the same as yours!" He cried, trying to get a look at his wife's meter. But Amelia took off as fast as she could. She screamed "Help!" at the top of her lungs, knowing full well that no one was around to hear her. Angus gave chase, but all those years of chicken schnitzel and mash and no veggies added many a kilo. He was too out-of-shape to keep pace with her and soon fell behind.

Angus slowed down as the heat rose. From where they were in the desert, not even an Olympic sprinter could have reached the resort in time. In exactly 10 minutes, he was collapsed on the dusty dirt of the Inferno Outback, dead.

Amelia turned around to see Angus' corpse. She checked her watch; she still had plenty of time, so she hurried back to him. She took the suit's various tubing, finding the spots she had punctured, and yanked them out. She pulled and scratched at it as hard as she could, and after a few minutes the pin-sized holes were the size of an old two-dollar Australian coin.

Amelia's task, however, still wasn't finished.

She took Angus' gloves off, his skin already burning, and put his hands on as many parts of the tubing as possible, getting his fingerprints all over it. She was thankful for her suit, which ensured that none of her prints would be anywhere on him. She was also thankful that his hands hadn't yet burned so badly that his fingerprints were scoured off. She did this until she could no longer stand to look at his red, raw skin. She glanced down at her watch and saw that she had plenty of time but decided that she'd tampered with the evidence enough. She got up and headed back to the resort to play the part of the distraught wife.

The next day, the authorities were called in from nearby Oak Valley to recover the body, or what was left of it. A quick autopsy declared that Angus died of 'circumstances attributed to the actions of the victim.' They gave Amelia the autopsy paperwork, and she requested a cremation which occurred an hour afterwards. She received the ashes of her husband to take back with her to Yorkers Pine Beach.

Amelia checked out of the hotel without paying. The resort insisted. As she drove home, she stopped by a roadside sign and opened the container of her husband's ashes. She poured them out unceremoniously, giving the bottom of the container a few vicious slaps to knock out the stubborn bits of him that remained.

Until death do us apart, she thought. When she was done disposing of Angus, she got back into the hovercraft with a big smile on her face.

"Well, we're apart now, Angus Kelly."

Accolades

Once upon a time in the quaint suburban neighbourhood of Northport, in New South Wales, Australia, there lived a man named Larry. Larry had always prided himself on being a good environmentalist. He read books, watched documentaries, and attended seminars about sustainability. Larry genuinely cared about the planet and its future, but there was one problem—he struggled to be an eco-conscious person at home.

Larry's journey towards environmentalism had started years ago, when he watched a documentary about the devastating effects of plastic pollution on marine life. The images of helpless turtles tangled in discarded fishing nets haunted him, and from that moment on, he vowed to do his part to protect the environment.

At first, Larry's efforts were commendable. He diligently carried a reusable water bottle, sorted his recyclables, and even started a small vegetable garden in his backyard. He was proud of his eco-friendly choices and believed he was making a difference. However, as time went on, he found it increasingly challenging to maintain his green lifestyle at home.

One day, as he stood in front of his overflowing trash can, Larry couldn't help but feel a twinge of guilt. His recycling bins were full of plastic bottles and cardboard boxes, but he couldn't remember the last time he'd composted or done anything to reduce his waste. He sighed and made a mental note to be more mindful.

The next morning, Larry noticed a leaky faucet in his bathroom. The constant dripping annoyed him, and he knew it was a waste of water. He tried to fix it, but his lack of plumbing skills only made matters worse. In the end, he was drenched in water and had to call a plumber, who replaced the entire faucet. Larry felt embarrassed about the water he'd wasted and his inability to make simple repairs.

Larry's most significant challenge was his love for convenience. He often succumbed to the allure of single-use products because they were easy. He stocked his kitchen with disposable plates, cups, and utensils, which he used far more often than his eco-friendly alternatives. He knew he should use reusable items, but the convenience of throwing things away was hard to resist. It was much less daunting a prospect than doing the dishes, and he told himself that he was really saving water by using paper plates, plastic silverware, and solo cups. Deep down, of course, he recognised that it was just an excuse.

One sunny afternoon, Larry took a walk to clear his mind. As he strolled through his neighbourhood, he noticed how vibrant and alive everything looked—the lush trees, the chirping birds, the well-maintained gardens of his neighbours. He couldn't help but contrast this with his bad habits at home and the waste he created. There was so much beauty in the world, and he was actively hampering it. He was contributing to wasteful, disgusting landfills. He didn't want to be part of the problem; he wanted to be part of the solution.

Feeling a renewed sense of purpose, Larry returned from his walk determined to make a change. He went farther than he'd ever gone before, even at the beginning when his eco-friendly lifestyle was so full of promise. He researched ways to reduce his waste, conserve water, and lower his carbon footprint. He enrolled in classes to learn basic home maintenance skills and vowed to fix any minor home issues himself. Slowly but surely, he transformed his house into an eco-friendlier space.

Larry started composting, switched to energy-efficient appliances, and grew more of his own food. He even inspired some of his neighbours to make eco-conscious choices of their own. Over time, his house became a model of sustainability, a reflection of his dedication to the environment.

As Larry looked out at his flourishing garden one evening, he couldn't help but smile. He had finally reconciled his desire to be a good environmentalist with his life at home. While the journey had been challenging, it had taught him that every small action counted, and that change began with personal commitment. However, there was one thing that bothered him, no matter how much he tried to ignore it: the nagging voice in his head that told him he deserved more than he got. He won no accolades, only personal satisfaction. He had only himself to share his success with. Even the neighbours he'd helped were too busy with their own green journeys to care much for his.

As Larry continued enjoying his garden, trying to keep selfish thoughts at bay, he heard a knock on his front door. He looks at his watch; it was later than any reasonable person would be knocking on doors. He wondered who it could be with a mixture of curiosity and annoyance.

Opening the door, Larry found a mature, regal woman with a serene and timeless beauty. She wore a vibrant dress with elements of the natural world, such as leaves and flowers, which she also had in her hair. Her attire mimicked the colours and textures of the Earth and its elements: green for lush forests, blue for serene waters and brown for fertile soil. She exuded a wisdom, tranquillity, and maternal care. Her gaze was nurturing and compassionate, and as her eyes fell on him, Larry felt a warmth rush through him as if it was the middle of the day.

Larry also noticed that the woman was carrying a staff. *Maybe it's a sceptre*, he thought. It was made of wood and had several crystals embedded into winding branches at the top. They radiated a pale blue light.

"May I help you?" Larry asked the woman as he stood in the threshold of his home.

"No, Larry. I am here to say thank you."

"To say thank you?"

"Yes, Larry, for all the wonderful work you have done in striving to be as sustainable as possible."

Larry blinked in confusion. He was more gratified by this than he let on, but the whole thing was so bizarre that he didn't dwell on his satisfaction. He'd never seen this woman before in his life; she could just as easily be a cosplayer as an environmentalist impressed by how he'd turned his life around. And how could she have known about that, anyway?

"I'm sorry, but who are you?" He asked.

"I am Mother Nature. No need to trouble yourself on my account; I am simply here to show my appreciation. Did you really think all your hard work on my behalf went unnoticed?" With that, the woman stepped into his house, wrapped him tight in a long embrace, and whispered "thank you" into his ear. Then she broke away and disappeared into the waning evening light.

Larry did not say or do anything this entire time. He was stunned into stillness.

"Who would believe me even if I told them?" He muttered to himself, staring at the spot where he had last seen Mother Nature. When he finally composed himself enough to move, he shut the door and, in the privacy of his own home, let a massive grin come over his face.

I couldn't have hoped for a better accolade than a visit from Mother Nature herself.

Spanked

Illuka and Warrin had always been best friends, their bond as enduring as the sands of the Sturt Stony desert they called home. Life was simple, but harsh. The two boys often ventured into the endless expanse of the desert, seeking adventure and escape from the monotony of their daily chores.

One scorching morning, with the sun beating down on the vast arid and semi-arid desert dominated by chenopod and acacia shrub lands, the more adventurous Warrin convinced Illuka to join him on an expedition to explore the parts of the desert they have never visited. They filled their canteens, packed a few provisions, and with their faces covered by headscarves to shield them from the biting sand, they set off.

As they trekked deeper into the desolate landscape, entering uncharted territory, the boys noticed peculiar patterns etched in the sand. These weren't the typical tracks left by desert creatures, but intricate and mysterious symbols that seemed to lead them somewhere. They couldn't resist following these unusual marks, their curiosity piqued.

After hours of walking, they reached a colossal rock formation jutting out of the desert like a forgotten monument. At its base, the intricate symbols converged into a circular pattern, and at the center of the circle lay a large, ornate key made of copper. Illuka and Warrin couldn't believe their eyes. The key was just as amazing as the symbols and rocks; they didn't think that anyone had ever been out here.

The key's otherworldly design was impossibly alluring, and Warrin cautiously reached for it. It was unlike anything they had ever seen in their modest village. The moment Warrin touched the key, the ground trembled beneath them, and the rock formation shifted. The boys hastily stepped back, their hearts pounding with a mixture of excitement and trepidation.

"What have you done Warrin?" Exclaimed Illuka.

With a deep, rumbling groan, the massive rock revealed a hidden entrance leading underground.

"Look at that, brother," stated Warrin. "That must be a passage."

Fuelled by his wild, adventurous spirit, he signalled to Illuka to venture into the darkness. He clutched the copper key tight to his chest as he descended into the hidden path, his more cautious friend in tow. Strangely, the boys found torches lining the tunnel, their flames dancing and casting eerie shadows on the walls. They continued onwards, their excitement increasing with each step. Illuka was becoming bolder and hurried to catch up to Warrin.

The tunnel led them into a vast underground chamber, where they found the most bizarre piece of equipment either boy had ever seen. A complex network of intertwining metallic tendrils were suspended in the center of a transparent, crystalline chamber of unknown origin. The device defied Warrin's and Illuka's school teachings by floating weightlessly, unbound by the laws of gravity.

Warrin and Illuka inched closer and read the fine etching on it. It said *Astral Seraphic Interstellar Propulsion Array.*

Illuka and Warrin look at each other, completely gobsmacked.

"Warrin, what do you think it does?"

"What, you can't read? It says it's an interstellar propulsion array."

"Yeah, I can read. What does it do?"

Warrin shrugged his shoulders, not knowing how to answer. He could make out the words, but their meaning was no clearer to him than it was to his friend. After trying in vain to figure it out, the boys continued investigating the chamber. Soon, they found what seemed to be a TV screen with two buttons on it, one green and one black.

They look at each other, as if confirming with each other what they both wanted to do. Boys being boys, Illuka nodded, and Warrin punched the green button. The screen lit up to show an alien-looking creature. It is tall and skeletal with a recognizable head and glowing orbs for eyes. Sound came through the device; the creature was speaking in a strange language.

"Brother, what did you do? What's that thing saying?" Asked a worried Illuka. Again, Warrin shrugged. The friends kept listening to the words, whose meaning they could not begin to fathom, and eventually Warrin pushed the black button in the hopes that something different would happen. The screen shut off for a moment and then came back on. The alien was there, and it began speaking like last time, but now it spoke in a language the boys could understand.

"Greetings, people of this strange and backward world. We stopped by a while back and saw how poorly developed your planet is. We took pity on you and decided to hasten the progression and development of your species. We are leaving you the Astral Seraphic Interstellar Propulsion Array as a means for you to join the Universal Federation of Planets. I am sure this comes as quite a shock, so when you are ready, ask me any questions you may have."

Once again, the boys looked at each other and wondered what they have gotten themselves into. And again, it was Warrin who acted first.

"Sir, what is this and what does it do?" He asked.

The alien on the TV replied: "The Astral Seraphic Interstellar Propulsion Array is a truly remarkable and enigmatic apparatus, a marvel of innovative technology that defies conventional aesthetics and engineering principles. Designed for the audacious purpose of enabling interstellar travel, this extraordinary contraption will allow the inhabitants of this backward planet to explore the cosmos."

"Brother, we're in trouble now," Illuka murmured softly. Unlike Warrin, who listened to the alien in awe, his response seemed to be chiefly one of fear.

"Why would we be in trouble? We didn't do anything wrong."

"We're doing something wrong by being here! We're not supposed to venture this far into the dessert. My parents are gonna kill me."

"Relax, Illuka. We'll go back home soon, and they'll have no idea where we were. Just let me ask a few more questions." Illuka said nothing in response, and Warrin took his friend's silence for assent.

"Sir, how does this contraption work?"

"At the center of this interstellar propulsion device lies a mesmerizing arrangement of concentric rings, glowing with an enchanting luminescence. Made from an extremely dense and unique alloy, the rings have unparalleled properties and will stand the test of time. Each ring spins at a different rate, resulting in a captivating optical illusion of constantly changing shapes. The Astral Seraphic Interstellar Propulsion Array has holographic displays embedded in the crystalline casing, allowing the user to manipulate the rings. Their spin and alignment can be changed in ways that bend the fabric of space-time, creating wormholes and warp fields. Once you read the instructions, you will see how simple it is. It is such a convenient method of travel; we marvel that your species has not yet invented a similar device!"

There was something arrogant in the alien's tone, but Warrin and Illuka were not paying attention. They were struggling just to wrap their heads around this miraculous technology, and the alien's explanation created more question than answers. Heedless of their confusion, however, the being on the screen continued.

"The Astral Seraphic Interstellar Propulsion Array operates on an enigmatic, zero-point energy source that draws power from the very essence of the universe. It emits a faint, ethereal hum, akin to the song of a celestial choir, as it charges up for an interstellar voyage. Again, it is all quite simple once you learn the instructions." That was the extent of the alien's answers, and neither of the boys asked it any more questions. Some of the words and phrases the creature used, even in their own language, were strange to their ears; they had never heard them before. What was a *zero-point energy source*? What did it mean to *draw power from the essence of the universe*? These questions and more kept Illuka silent. He and Warrin understood that this Astral Seraphic Interstellar Propulsion Array was an engine of sorts, but he couldn't fathom what it might be used for other than flying through space, which didn't seem all that remarkable considering that humans already had satellites and rocket ships and Mars Rovers.

Warrin came to these same conclusions, but he saw something Illuka didn't: an opportunity to make some money.

"Illuka, we just discovered an alien and its ship. This place is gonna be famous; people will come here from all over to go into space."

"So?"

"Our families can take them there! We get our parents to come here, they can read the instructions and fly this thing. Millionaires and billionaires all wanna go to space, and we can be the ones to take them…if they pay up."

Illuka just stared at his friend, taking this all in. He thought for an objection, feeling that it couldn't possibly be this easy.

"Who's gonna run it? My old man doesn't know shit about engines. Does yours?"

Warrin realised Illuka had a point, but he was undeterred. This time, it was his turn to stop and think.; there had to be another way to exploit this device. It was too valuable to just leave here for someone else to find, and Warrin wouldn't be able to live with himself if he abandoned it and someone else found it and made a fortune ferrying people into space.

"We'll sell it to the Americans. You know they have science guys," he said, finally coming up with another idea.

"Who?"

"Their science guys! You know, the ones we read about in school. The ones that said: 'Houston, we have a problem.'"

"Oh, yeah. They know about flying into space. Or we could sell to the Chinese. I heard they have a lot of money. Maybe they'll pay more." Illuka was starting to get bolder. His friend's opportunism was rubbing off on him. Warrin considered this suggestion, and for a few moments, it seemed like a good idea. He'd heard the same thing about the Chinese. He heard their economy was doing great, and that it might be even better than America's. Then he shook his head.

"No, we sell it to the Americans. I like their hot dogs. I don't like chop suey."

Illuka thought about that for a moment before nodding.

"You're right. Hot dogs are the best. Let's sell to the Americans."

"Awesome!"

The boys shook on their deal to sell the Astral Seraphic Interstellar Propulsion Array to the Americans. They furiously pumped their arms up and down, moving so excitedly that it looked to anyone watching like they were both trying to tear the other's arm out of its socket.

"What are you gonna do with the money you make from the sale?" Asked an excited Illuka.

"I'll buy a Xbox Series X or PS5. Hell, maybe I'll buy both! What about you?"

"I'm getting the MeekBoyz Downhill bike!"

"That's so cool. You can use my consoles if I get to ride your bike," said Warrin.

"Deal!"

The boys continued to talk excitedly about their future purchases. A few minutes passed in jubilant anticipation until their conversation ran its course and they realised they were still in the underground passage. Warrin looked down and saw the key still in his hand.

"What else does the key do?" Illuka asked.

"Well, it opens the passage, so it probably closes it too. Other than that, no idea."

"Ask the alien. It probably knows."

The idea made so much sense that Warrin wished he'd thought of it first.

"Sir, what does the key do besides open the passage?" He asked.

For the first time, the alien looked surprised. Still, it answered the question all the same.

"It turns on the Astral Seraphic Interstellar Propulsion Array, of course. You insert it here." It pointed to a holographic keyhole that appeared beside the floating device and spoke matter-of-factly, as if its reply was the most obvious thing in the entire word. Warrin felt a little embarrassed and tentatively walked towards the Astral Seraphic Interstellar Propulsion Array. When he was close enough, he inserted the key into the hologram and turned it.

Suddenly the device began to spin rapidly, and in the blink of an eye Warrin and Illuka found themselves in space. They looked around, hardly able to take in the fact that the rock formation they found was really the body of their newly acquired interstellar spacecraft before it rocketed off, hurtling through space on a journey to an undisclosed location.

"Warrin, what did you do? We're in space! Where are we going? Were we in a spaceship the whole time?" Illuka shot off questions like a machine gun fired bullets.

"I don't know, Illuka. But I do know one thing."

"What's that?"

"You're not getting that MeekBoyz Downhill bike, and I'm not getting an Xbox Series X or PS5. You know what we're getting?"

"What?"

"Spanked. We're getting spanked when we get back home."

143

Unpredictable Skies

The Stuart family, comprising John, his wife Mary, and their three daughters, lived a peaceful life in a cozy suburban home in Northport, New South Wales.

John's grandfather had immigrated from the United States in the late 1870s and had bought a large block of land of what was, at the time, nothing more than cow pasture. Robert Stuart was a savvy investor and could make a good case for being a psychic, as he predicted that the land would double and even triple in value. He took monumental financial risks, and everyone was certain he would fall to ruin, but instead he brought prosperity to his land and family. Robert put all his time and effort into building his home for his family and had successfully paid off his mortgage by late 1889. He had a house all his own, one he could pass down through the generations.

Then came the crash.

In 1891, land values fell to about one-half their boom levels. In the suburb of Camden, for instance, prices peaked at an average of more than £1,000 per property in 1888 and fell to £520 in 1898.

Robert, remarkably, was unaffected. His preternatural business savvy shielded him and his family. While many people lost their homes, he expanded his. And that wasn't the only bizarre move he made. He did something that was more than a little strange by Australian standards at the time: he built a new, larger home on his property with a basement.

Once the new house was built, people who had curiously looked on during the construction process would knock on his door and ask Robert to give them a peek into the basement, and he gladly obliged. It made him the talk of the town, and he was happy to show off the fruit of his labours.

Little did Robert know just how useful it would be for his descendants.

One summer evening, as John, Mary and the girls gathered in the media room to watch the news, they realised right away that their lives were about to take an unexpected turn.

The news anchor's face was scrunched up in consternation as she reported on bizarre weather patterns across the globe. The whole natural order seemed to have been upended. In Georgia, USA, it was snowing heavily in the middle of July, while in the Indian town of Dras, the temperature had dropped to minus 45 degrees Celsius. Earthquakes and tsunamis were happening in places where they had never occurred before. Chaos was gripping the planet.

The family exchanged worried glances, and John's voice quavered as he said, "We need to prepare for the worst."

With that, they rushed to the basement and gathered supplies of canned food, bottled water, blankets, flashlights, and a battery-powered radio. Their daughters, Lily, Emily, and Sophie, packed as much as they could into their school backpacks. All three had a mix of curiosity and fear on their faces as they follow their father's instruction.

Once they collected all the supplies, the family huddled together in their basement sanctuary, listening to the eerie sounds of unpredictable weather outside. It had reached them. They knew they needed a plan.

"John, what are we going to do?" Asked Mary.

"We can't do anything, not with what's happening out there. The utilities won't work in this crazy weather. We just have to stay here and hope for the best. Girls, did you grab all the spare batteries like I asked?"

The three girls nodded their heads, almost in unison.

"Mary, what about food? How much do we have?"

"I packed ten large bags with pasta, beans, rice, protein bars, and black beans and beef stew. They're heavy, but the girls are strong. They should each be able to carry two, and we can get the rest."

"It's nothing fancy, but we should be able to live off that until we find food."

"How do we find food?" Asked Sophie, the youngest. John smiled at her reassuringly but said nothing. He had no idea.

They spent a day in the basement, and while it kept the family safe, the girls were already growing antsy. He only needed the one day to know that they couldn't stay down in the basement, not forever, and especially not since they lost power almost immediately after the violent weather had come their way. They could either starve or lose their minds in here, or go up and find, against all odds, a more permanent shelter.

John chose the latter. He explained to his family that their best chance was to head for the mountains, hoping to find some semblance of safety and stability there. With backpacks and bags filled and their hearts heavy, he, Mary and the girls ventured out into the now-chaotic world.

The sky was a swirling canvas of bizarre, alternating weather phenomena. Lightning without thunder, rainbows at night, erratic winds. Nature seemed to have lost its balance.

Their journey was fraught with challenges. They encountered washed out roads and collapsed bridges. They came across desperate people along the way, all searching for safety and answers in a world turned upside down. The Stuarts shared some of their supplies with those they met, and they received advice and information about the rapidly changing weather patterns. Some of these people joined them on their trek to the mountains.

After several gruelling days, the Stuarts and their retinue finally reached the foothills of the mountains. Here, the weather seemed less erratic, and the air was crisp and cool. John's hunch had been right. He thought that perhaps, like his grandfather, he had a touch of ESP. They set up camp, hoping that higher ground would provide them with some protection from the unpredictable weather. Their little group of five had now grown to 34, with six additional families joining the Stuarts along the way.

Days turned into weeks as the Stuarts and the other families adapted to their new reality. They learned to read the ever-shifting weather patterns, predicting when it was safe to venture out for supplies and when to seek shelter. They built a close-knit community, sharing skills and knowledge to survive in the strange world more deadly than anything they'd ever known.

As months passed, scientists around the globe worked tirelessly to understand the cause of the weather upheaval and restore balance to the planet. In the early days, radios were buzzing with transmissions, and anyone could, more likely than not, listen in on the scientists' communications by tuning into a random station. Even in their panic and uncertainty, they were a source of comfort to the beleaguered Stuarts and their retinue; their voices were a sign that there were people out there working to save them, to save their place on the planet.

It didn't last. It became increasingly clear to those who cared to listen that the scientists had no answers, and slowly their transmissions decreased in frequency. Eventually, they stopped altogether. Radio silence. The Stuarts and the families who came with them had no contact with anywhere else in the world. Just each other.

The day that they turned on the radio and found every single channel empty, a sadness settled over them. They looked at each other and saw hopelessness written on their haggard faces.

"Are we doomed, John?" Asked Paul Peterson. All the people around him looked at John too. He had become the de facto leader of their retinue. When no one else had any answers, they sought his. He always had one.

"No," was all that John said. Paul's expression lifted a bit; his frown softened, and he stood up straighter. He, along with everyone else, took heart in John's single word. It gave them hope, and they clung to that hope tight, believing that humanity's resilience and determination would eventually prevail over the tempestuousness of nature.

It was not to be.

One evening, while the community was huddled together sharing the warmth of a campfire, they heard a loud crack of thunder. They all looked up to the sky and gasped, their voices mingling into a massive intake of breath.

A fireball was hurting straight towards the mountain.

John knew from the size of it that it would cause an extinction event when it hit the earth. Only the hardiest of living things would survive, and that did not include humanity. He gathered his family close to him and encouraged the others to do the same. However, most of them lost their composure when they say the sky alight with flame. Their hope was snuffed out, replaced with fear. They fled into nearby caves, seeking shelter anywhere they could, but John knew; there was no escaping this end.

Amid the chaos of the community's flight and the fireball growing closer and closer, its heat touching the skin of all who stood or fled, John knew that he and his family had found strength in their love. As they looked up at their extinction, they knew that while the world would end soon, their love and determination to protect each other never would. It would remain long after their bodies were reduced to ash, stalwart even as the unpredictable skies brought the end to humanity.

The E-Phone 26 Conspiracy

The morning sun rose over the city of Sydney, casting its golden glow upon the towering skyscrapers and Harbour Bridge. It was a day like any other, or so it seemed. But little did the world know, the unlikeliest of incidents would throw the world into chaos.

In the heart of the central business district (CBD), special CIA agent Brent Walker stood on the rooftop of an inconspicuous building overlooking the Darling Harbour. He had received a cryptic message late the previous night that hinted at an impending global catastrophe. It mentioned the e-Phone 26, believed to be the most secure smartphone ever created.

As the morning progressed, news started pouring in from around the world. Reports of assassinations of key political leaders in countries like the United States, Russia, China, and France started to come in. Panic spread like wildfire as governments struggled to grasp the enormity of the situation. The world was on the brink of an unprecedented crisis.

Brent's phone buzzed with an urgent call from his superior, Director Samantha Foster. She was at the Australian Secret Intelligence Service (ASIS) headquarters in Canberra, coordinating the global response.

"Brent, we believe this is no coincidence. We've found evidence that someone hacked the e-Phone 26, allowing them to detonate it remotely," Samantha said, her voice trembling with concern.

Brent knew he had to act quickly. He made his way to a secret facility that still had an uncompromised e-Phone 26. With the help of a brilliant tech expert, Dr. Elena Ramirez, he delved into the phone's code.

Hours turned into days as they worked tirelessly to decipher the intricate layers of the hack. It became clear the perpetrators possessed a level of sophistication that suggested state-sponsored involvement. Brent and Elena followed a trail of digital breadcrumbs that led them to a shadowy organization known as 'Tech-Reapers.' This secretive group of hackers had a history of targeting global leaders to destabilize nations. They were notorious for their ability to stay hidden in the darkest corners of the internet.

As they dug deeper, Brent and Elena uncovered an unexpected ally—an inside source who had become disillusioned with the organization's intentions. This informant, codenamed 'Whistle,' provided crucial information that brought them closer to identifying the culprits.

Their pursuit led them to an abandoned factory on the outskirts of Northport, a suburb just seventy-five kilometres south of Sydney. It was there they discovered a single computer, with tons of monitors and lots of empty Red Rock Sweet Chilli potato chips bags.

Brent and his team hid and waited. They had reason to believe that the leader of the Tech-Reapers, an enigmatic figure known as 'The Maestro,' was due to make an appearance at the factory.

Their wait wasn't long. Soon, The Maestro walked in, sat in front of the monitors, and opened a bag of potato chips. That was their cue; Brent's team pounced.

The Maestro shot to his feet, screamed, and started crying at the sight of the handguns and machine guns aimed at him. At twelve years of age, Matthew Caruso Zocco—Matty to his friends—had never been in trouble.

Brent immediately ordered his team to stand down. The Maestro was just a kid, holding nothing more dangerous than a bag of cheap junk food. He was a CIA agent, not a childcare professional, but his training kicked in and he knew he had to calm the kid down to get an answer out of him. Ordering his team to leave, Brent sat down with Matty, one-on-one, and waited till the boy was calm enough to answer questions.

"Why did you target the e-Phone 26, Matty?" He asked.

"I hate the e-Phone 26. They're so expensive and my parents won't get me one!" Matty replied angrily, between sniffles.

"But why did you join the Tech Reapers? They're an incredibly dangerous group."

Matty shrugged.

"I thought it would be fun. They said I was really good, and they wanted to work with me. Then they wanted me to be in charge. None of them can code like I can."

"And your codename? The Maestro?"

"I took it from a video game."

Brent rubbed the bridge of his nose with his fingers, sighing in exasperation. Nothing about this boy screamed black hat hacker or violent anti-government revolutionary. He couldn't fathom why this kid would use his hatred of the e-Phone 26 to kill world leaders.

"Matty, why did you program them to explode?"

The boy's eyes went wide.

"I didn't. I just wanted to blow up the code. You know, delete it so no one could use their stupid phones."

Brent hid his surprise much better than Matty. The boy had no idea what he'd done. Brent considered revealing to Matty the consequences of his childish actions—the deaths of many world leaders and the destabilisation of the international community. But that seemed cruel, and he would learn soon enough, anyway. Brent was a man on a mission, and right now, that mission was to get answers.

"So, you never intended to hurt anyone?" He asked.

"No! I'm sorry if I did, but I need to go home now. I'm late for dinner and my parents are gonna kill me."

"Before you go, I need you to remove all the malicious code in all the remaining e-Phones. Can you do that, Matty?" Brent asked. The boy nodded, and the agent motioned for him to go to his computer and get to work. It only took a few keystrokes, and in less than a minute, he turned to Brent and said, "Done."

His mission complete, Brent reported to his superior that they had captured The Maestro and secured the remaining e-Phones, guaranteeing that there would be no more explosions. He was reluctant to admit that The Maestro, the mysterious figure who nearly brought down the entire global order, was just a kid whose parents wouldn't let him have a phone, but when he did, Ms Foster suggested Brent take Matty back to his parents and explain what happen.

Brent obeyed his superior's orders. When he brought Matty back to his parents, he was surprised by how normal the Zocco household seemed. Nothing he saw indicated that Matty was anything more than a spoiled kid with a genius intellect and too much time on his hands. His parents, however, struck Brent as odd. Well, one of them. Matty's mom was horrified and got through the conversation in a state of shock, unable to comprehend that her son could do something so horrible just by messing with some code. She clutched him tight the entire time, as if afraid he'd run off and cause another global catastrophe. His dad, John, was another story.

John was oddly disinterested in his son's actions and welfare; instead, he kept asking questions about what the world governments were going to do. Brent kept answering that he did not know but wondered at John's composure throughout their talk. He seemed more concerned about the e-Phone than his own son. Being a single man, Brent put little thought into it then. He supposed that this was just how fathers were; his own dad hadn't been much more attentive.

Later, Brent put two and two together.

With the crisis averted, the world leaders who had survived the assassination attempts came together to strengthen international cybersecurity measures. They recognised the need for unprecedented cooperation to prevent such a catastrophe from happening again. Fearful of what all the world's budding tech geniuses could do given the time and motivation, the international community decided they would provide free e-Phones to all children in the world once they reached the age of 12.

Brent Walker had saved the world from the brink of chaos, but in doing so, he had just handed Matty's father a golden egg.

The *Financial Review* reported that in the weeks following the 'The e-Phone Conspiracy,' as it came to be known, a mysterious company had placed a spread bet counting on the maker of the e-Phone's share price skyrocketing with the announcement made by the global community. Sure enough, the company became the most successful in the world, as governments across the globe placed huge orders for e-Phone 26s to send to their country's 12-year-olds.

A few weeks later, Australian Federal Police knocked on the Zocco family's door and charged Matty's father with a conspiracy to defraud the e-Phone maker by manipulating the share market.

In the digital age, new threats would continue to emerge, and Brent was committed to protecting his country and the world from those who sought to use technology for evil.

The e-Phone 26 incident served as a stark reminder that in an interconnected world, the line between honesty and corruption was thinner than ever before. It was a lesson the world and agent Brent Walker would never forget.

You Can't Always Get What You Want

Northport, New South Wales, is a quaint little town nestled between rolling hills and babbling brooks. It is known for many things, including an affinity for recycling. One member of this idyllic community, however, took it more seriously than all the rest.

Paul Marj was a rather eccentric fellow, known for his peculiar habits and even stranger ideas. His latest fascination? Recycling himself.

You see, Paul had always been passionate about environmental conservation. He wanted to be the best at recycling and recycled everything from plastic bottles to old newspapers. He even took it upon himself to pick up litter on the streets, much to the amusement of the townsfolk. Paul interrupted many a council meeting to interject with some solution to the recycling issue, and due to his bullishness, he always got what he wanted.

But Paul wasn't satisfied, and one sunny morning, he decided to take his eco-friendly endeavours to a whole new level. Paul invited his neighbours to his backyard, where he had set up a device straight out of a science fiction novel. It comprised a complex assembly of gears and levers, with a large, mysterious contraption in the center. He explained to the puzzled crowd that he was going to recycle himself to reduce his carbon footprint.

His neighbour, Mrs Jenkins, raised an eyebrow and asked, "Paul, are you sure about this? Recycling is great, but I think you might be taking it a bit too far."

Paul, undeterred, reassured her. "Don't worry, Mrs Jenkins. I've done extensive research on this. I'll emerge from this process as a lean recycling machine! People will be red with envy."

With that, he climbed onto a platform at the heart of the contraption, donned a piece of headgear that looked like a cross between a bicycle helmet and a spacesuit, and pressed a big, red button. The contraption sprang to life, humming and whirring as sparks flew in all directions.

The onlookers watched in both awe and amusement as Paul's body began to twitch and convulse. Then, with a flash of blinding light and a cloud of smoke, he disappeared. The contraption fell silent, its gears grinding to a halt. In his sudden absence, the crowd was left standing there, flabbergasted.

For a moment, the townsfolk were too stunned to react, but then they burst into laughter. It was the strangest thing they had ever seen! Mrs Jenkins couldn't help but chuckle.

"Well, I suppose he's reduced his carbon footprint to zero now!"

Days turned into weeks, and Paul was nowhere to be found. The town continued to buzz with rumours and jokes about his mysterious recycling experiment. Some believed he had turned into a talking recycling bin, while others thought he was living in a secret underground lair, composting his way to eco-superhero status.

Then, one sunny afternoon, as the townsfolk were gathered in the park for a community clean-up event, they heard a familiar, but sad, voice.

It was Paul!

Or at least someone who sounded like him, coming from a nearby rubbish bin.

"Hi, everyone! It's me, Paul! I've become one with the red rubbish bin! It's not exactly what I wanted, for I don't get to do much recycling. Most of the stuff in me goes to the landfill."

Then, in a much cheerier voice, Pauls said: "I'm here to remind you to recycle your plastic bottles and paper!"

The townsfolk couldn't believe their ears. Paul had indeed become a talking bin, just not the one he'd hoped for.

From that day on, Paul the Red Bin became a beloved fixture in the town, reminding everyone to recycle and reduce their waste each time someone dumped a half-eaten hamburger in him.

And so, in the quirky little town between the hills and brooks, the townsfolk learned that sometimes, a little eccentricity could bring about the worst, most unexpected and eco-friendly transformations.

Like the old song goes: *You can't always get what you want.*

Making Millions

Sally, the Atlantic salmon, and Tony the tuna had been inseparable friends for as long as they could remember. They swam together through the vast depths of the Atlantic Ocean, sharing stories and adventures in the blue expanse. But on one fateful day, as they glided effortlessly through the water, they put their friendship to the ultimate test.

As Sally and Tony ventured deeper into the ocean, they came across a heartbreaking sight: Tommy the turtle, a wise and gentle creature, was ensnared in a web of fishing lines. His usually serene eyes were filled with panic as he writhed to free himself, his flippers tangled in the cruel strings of human activity.

The friends exchanged worried glances. They knew they had to do something. Their little fishy hearts broke as the watched Tommy's futile struggling, and the two friends swam up to the gentle creature.

"Don't worry, Tommy. We're here to help," Sally whispered.

Tony added, "We'll get you out of this. Just stay calm."

Tommy, surprised and grateful, nodded. Together, the trio worked tirelessly to free him from the entangled mess. Sally carefully tried to loosen the lines using her powerful tail, while Tony navigated the intricate knots with his agility. But they were unsuccessful.

As they laboured in vain, a curious thing happened.

Two nearby humans in a fishing boat noticed the unusual behaviour of the aquatic trio. They had never seen fish and a turtle working together in such a coordinated manner. Intrigued, they peered into the water. When they saw Sally and Tony appearing to communicate with Tommy, their astonishment knew no bounds. They moved their boat closer to get a better look.

The disturbance they created in the water caught Sally and Tony's attention. At first, they were terrified. They couldn't get Tommy free, and now a group of humans were here to catch them. They worked frantically in a last-ditch effort to untangle Tommy from his bonds before the humans could get them, but strangely, the two-legged beings did not move. They just watched Sally and Tony work, transfixed.

This gave the friends an idea—a desperate one, to be sure, but desperation was all they had. Their bodies may not have been suited to free Tommy, but the humans, whose hands created the horrors that bound the sea turtle, could save him. They just had to ask.

Sally and Tony were going to break the unspoken law by which all aquatic creatures lived: the rule of silence. It was a code that forbade them from ever speaking to humans, for fear of the consequences it might bring to their underwater world. But if they didn't ask, they feared the consequences it might bring to Tommy.

Sally said to Tony: "Can you swim up and tell them we need help?"

"Righty oh, Sally," replied Tony. Quick as a flash, he swam towards the boat. When he reached the fishermen, Tony screamed at the top of his gills.

"Please help our friend, Tommy! He is all tangled up and we cannot free him!"

"Did you hear that, Jack? The tuna spoke to us," one of the fishermen said, bemused.

"He sure did, Peter." The one named Jack spoke slowly, and unbeknownst to Tony, picked up a net and hid it behind his back. Then, he turned to the tuna.

"Hi, you got a name?"

"Yes, kind sir. My name is Tony the tuna. Can you help us save our friend Tommy?"

"Tommy is the turtle, right?" asked Jack again.

"Yes sir. Will you help?"

"Tony, does the salmon have a name? Can it speak like you?" Jack pressed.

"She is my best friend Sally the salmon, and yes, she can speak. Will you help friend Tommy? Please, he is getting tired."

The two fishermen looked at each other for several moments, and Tony couldn't begin to guess what they were communicating with their gaze. Finally, however, Peter turned back to him.

"Come closer. We can't hear you."

Suddenly Tony heard a loud shout from Sally: "Hurry, Tony! Tommy is sinking. He cannot stay up anymore. He has gotten too tired. Please come!"

Tony immediately whipped back around and swam to her. The fishermen decide to follow, and Peter got the boat moving towards the three friends. As they drew closer, they saw that where there had once been three, there was now only two. The turtle was too tired to stay afloat and had drifted to the bottom of the ocean. Tony and Sally swam over to the fishermen as they approached, intending to thank them and implore them to hurry. The boat came to a halt, as if waiting for them. Once she was close enough, Sally thanked them first.

"Kind sirs. My name is Sally. My friend Tony and I thank you for—" Before she could finish, Peter scooped her and Tony out of the ocean with a net and threw them into a huge bucket of sea water.

"What is going on? What have you done?" Asked Tony, bewildered by this turn of events, but the fishermen did not respond. All they did was hoot and holler with glee.

"We're going to be rich, Petey-boy! Talking fish! We'll make millions! Now start the boat. We're going back to port."

With that, the fishermen set off, moving farther and farther from where Tommy the turtle was sinking deep into the ocean.

It took a couple of hours for the boat to reach port, and before they got to land, Jack leaned over Sally and Tony's bucket. Seeing his massive, scowling face from their bucket of water, which might as well have been a single drop compared to the vastness of the sea they called home, the two friends had never been more terrified.

"When we arrive at port, you'll speak only when we tell you to. If you don't do exactly what we say, we'll just fillet you and have you both for dinner. You understand?"

Simultaneously, they answered with a sad: "Yes, we do."

"Good," said Jack. He turned back to Peter.

Sally and Tony barely spoke afterwards, but when they did, they were so quiet that the fishermen did not hear them. Together, they came up with a plan.

Arriving at port, both Jack and Peter started screaming for people to come closer and hear the "crazy talking fish." People pulled out their phones and cameras, and waited for the moment the fish were to speak.

News of the talking fish spread like wildfire, however, and it drew far more than curious laypeople. Soon, reporters arrived with their own camera assistants. Then came marine biologists, environmentalists, and more media outlets. Some were there to record the event, while others were there to study and protect these remarkable creatures. They recognised the significance of this unique duo and wanted to raise awareness about safeguarding the ocean and its inhabitants.

The crowd grew to well over a hundred, and front and centre were the major television stations and some cable news networks. Sensing it was time, Jack came to the front of the crowd with the bucket of water holding Sally and Tony.

"Folks, we are humble fishermen, and we came upon these two beautiful specimens and heard their conversation. We thought we'd bring them here so all of you can witness this marvellous event. However, to bring this marvel to you, we had to sacrifice a day's worth of wages, or about $1,200.00. So, before I ask the fish to speak, my partner Peter will pass the hat. Please give us $5 or $10 to make up for our lost wages. I promise hearing these two speak will be well worth it."

There was some hesitation at first, but then someone said aloud: "Hell, $5 buys you a cup of coffee these days. That's worth hearing some fish talk." Then he approached Peter and threw a $5 note into the hat.

Others followed suit. Even the news reporters were giving the fishermen money. One of the policemen who had come to confirm the rumours looked at his Sargent, who nodded in the affirmative, and in went a $10 note.

After a few minutes, the hat was full. Peter, who had been counting as the money went in, nodded to Jack as if to say, 'we cleared more than enough' and stepped back to let him continue with the announcement.

"Ladies and gentlemen, we thank you for your support. Now let me introduce you to Sally the salmon and Tony the tuna!"

Nothing happened. Jack thought that perhaps the fish, with their tiny brains, didn't get the message. Looking straight at Sally and Tony, eyes narrowed, and mouth curled into a deep frown, Jack commanded: "Speak to the crowd." He added, so softly that no one else could hear, *or you'll be fillet tonight.*

"Move closer folks. They're kind of shy," Jack said as he turned back to the crowd and motioned the folks on the pier to come closer.

A few minutes passed, and still there was silence.

"Speak!" Screamed Jack as Peter moved closer to him.

Softly, Peter asked: "Jack, what's happening? Why aren't they talking?"

Once again, Jack commanded in an even louder voice: "Speak you two, or it'll be fish fillets for dinner!"

With that statement, a few of the environmentalist and conservationist groups move forward and grabbed the bucket containing the talking fish. At the same time, the constable and his Sargent grabbed the fishermen.

"Looks like you boys are going to be serving two to three years for fraud," said the Sargent.

"Fraud? It's not fraud! They speak! I tell you; we heard them!"

Someone proposed, "Why don't we go to the shore and let these two scared creatures go back to their natural environment?" Jack and Peter could only cry out in protest as they were loaded into a nearby police wagon.

The group of onlookers, in almost a single file line, marched down to the shore and let Sally and Tony swim out of the bucket and head off to sea.

When they were far away from shore, Tony said: "Wow, we almost did not make it, but your plan worked. Keeping silent sure made those two fishermen look foolish. How did you know?"

"Well Tony, just remember that these humans evolved from us, so we are just as smart as they are. Let's go home."

"Yes, let's go home."

And so, as Sally and Tony continued to swim home through the deep blue sea, they knew that their friendship had not only endured, but helped put two very nasty humans in jail.

"Making millions," scoffed Sally. "Doubt you two will make millions doing kitchen work in jail."

One Rotten Apple Spoils The Barrel

Charlie Hopkins was a passionate conservationist, dedicated to preserving the beauty of the natural world around him. His life was a testament to his commitment, from volunteering at the local wildlife sanctuary to leading community cleanup efforts. In his hometown of Northport, New South Wales, Charlie was known far and wide as a guardian of the environment. He even appeared on national television, and he was proud to be a symbol of conservation for others around the world—or at least Northport.

Charlie's day began like any other, with the warm rays of the sun streaming through his bedroom window. As he rolled out of bed and stretched, he couldn't help but smile at the thought of the new day and the potential it held for making a positive impact on the planet.

Downstairs, in his cozy kitchen, Charlie prepared a simple breakfast. He reached for a bright red apple from the fruit bowl, polished it with care, and took a satisfying bite. The crisp, sweet taste of the apple filled his senses. He ate it down to the core and prepared to compost it, but then the landline rang. In a moment of distraction, he tossed the apple core into the rubbish bin instead of the compost bin. It was an innocent mistake, one that anyone might make on a busy morning.

As the apple core lay in the trash, it decomposed, releasing a small amount of methane gas. Unbeknownst to

Charlie, this seemingly minor act would set off a chain of events that would change the course of history.

Under normal circumstances, the methane would have been absorbed by the Earth's natural processes. However, Northport had recently cut funding for landfill maintenance, and the gas capture system had fallen into disrepair.

Over weeks, the methane from the apple core seeped into the atmosphere, where it joined other greenhouse gases. It was just a tiny contribution to the growing climate crisis, but it was enough to tip the scales. Weather patterns became increasingly erratic, and extreme storms became the new norm. Glaciers melted at an alarming rate, causing sea levels to rise rapidly.

Charlie soon realised the gravity of his mistake, but it was too late. The world he had dedicated his life to protecting was spiralling into chaos. Desperate to make amends, he embarked on a mission to reverse the damage. He organized global campaigns, mobilized communities, and worked tirelessly to raise awareness about the dire consequences of climate change.

However, Charlie made another mistake. He told several reporters how his inadvertent miss had caused all this misery.

As the months passed, Charlie's efforts did not make a difference, and the world was forever changed. The once-stable climate had shifted irreversibly, leading to untold hardships for all of humanity. It was a harsh reminder that every action, no matter how small, could have far-reaching consequences.

People were in an uproar. Plans were already being implemented to leave planet Earth before humanity perished, but someone had to pay. The question was *who*.

Finding a scapegoat didn't take long. Someone in the press remembered Charlie's comment about his apple and reported him to the United Nations General council. The United Nations convened a special session. The representative from Australia's government was there, along with Charlie Hopkins himself.

Australia's United Nations representative fought hard for Charlie, to no avail. The world was dying because of his one mistake. The process was slow, and scientists estimated it would take months for the full effects to be felt, but the world was paying for Charlie's error.

The Secretary General of the United Nations made his announcement after hearing every country's input on Charlie Hopkins' lapse of judgment. He said: "Charlie Hopkins had been the embodiment of conservation, but in one thoughtless moment, he unwittingly contributed to the Earth's destruction. His story must be preserved, to serve as a poignant lesson for generations to come. His carelessness is a reminder that the fate of our planet rests in the hands of each and every one of us, and that even the smallest actions can have monumental consequences."

Taking a moment to look straight at Charlie, he concluded: "Charlie Hopkins, I sentence you to live the rest of your life in the very environment you helped destroy. You will be taken to a remote prison in your homeland and when humanity departs on the last spaceship to inhabit other planets, the locks of your prison will open, and we will leave you behind to fend for yourself in the harsh conditions you helped create. You will be the last human on a desolate planet, living alongside the remnants of any surviving life. May God have mercy on your soul."

As they lead Charlie away, he was reminded of an old adage: *one rotten apple spoils the barrel.*

Whispers Of the Past

In the year 2124, the world had changed in unimaginable ways. Some changes were for the better, while others were for the worse. Some things, however, remained as frustrating as ever. Adriana McDougal, a spirited young girl of 16 with dreams as big as the holographic billboards in the sky, was about to embark on a journey that would test her patience and resilience. She was going for her driver's license.

The year 2124 was full of self-driving cars, hoverboards, and teleportation devices, making the need for traditional driving skills almost obsolete. But Adriana was determined to get her license, for she believed that there was nothing quite like the thrill of driving a good old-fashioned car like they did in the old days. Alas, you hardly ever saw them on the road now.

As she walked into the sleek, ultra-modern building that housed the Service NSW Centre in Northport, Adriana couldn't help but feel a twinge of nostalgia for days she'd never known, when people used to drive manually. She approached the holographic receptionist, which looked suspiciously like a giant, floating smiley-face emoji.

"Hello, I'm here for my driver's test," Adriana said with a confident grin.

The holographic receptionist nodded and replied with a cheerful, "Sure thing! Here is your number on the queue. Just take a seat, and your instructor will be with you shortly."

Adriana sat down, her heart pounding with excitement. She imagined herself cruising through the futuristic city, with windblown hair and a smile that could outshine the neon lights. Little did she know her dreams were about to take a detour.

Her instructor, a robotic AI with a monotone voice and a distinct lack of humour, introduced himself as Instructor 4528. He had a face that only a motherboard could love.

"Hello, Adriana. Please enter the virtual driving simulator," Instructor 4528 said, motioning towards a holographic simulator hovercraft cockpit. Adriana eagerly climbed into the simulator and adjusted her virtual seatbelt. The futuristic car before her had buttons, switches, and screens galore.

Instructor 4528 explained the first task. "We will begin with a simple lane change. When I give the signal, please merge into the right lane."

Adriana nodded, ready to impress the mechanical instructor. She sped up, merging smoothly into the right lane. So far, so good.

But then, things took a turn for the absurd. A holographic giant two-headed cat appeared in the middle of the road, chasing a virtual laser pointer. Adriana swerved to avoid it, nearly hitting a holographic fire hydrant. She glanced at Instructor 4528, who simply stared back with robotic indifference.

"Uh, sorry about that. Cat on the road, you know?" Adriana offered, trying to make light of the situation.

Instructor 4528 didn't react, and the test continued. Next up, she had to navigate through a virtual traffic jam. Just when she thought she was doing well, a holographic clown car pulled up beside her. Clowns started pouring out, honking horns, and juggling bowling pins.

Adriana, both startled and amused, couldn't help but laugh. She swerved again, narrowly missing a clown on a unicycle. The virtual traffic jam turned into virtual chaos, and Instructor 4528's digital eyebrows seemed to raise in digital disappointment.

Finally, the test ended. Adriana parked the virtual car and awaited her fate. Instructor 4528's monotone voice broke the silence.

"I'm sorry, Adriana, but you have failed your driver's test. Your reactions to unexpected stimuli were inadequate, and your driving lacked precision."

Adriana sighed, realizing that perhaps her dreams of becoming a legendary future driver were a bit too ambitious. She stepped out of the simulator, determined to try again.

As she left the Service Centre, she couldn't help but chuckle. In 2124, even the driver's tests had evolved into something utterly bizarre. But Adriana McDougal was not one to give up easily.

As she was walking out, she noticed the car museum that was next to the Service NSW Centre. *Funny, I didn't see it when I was going into the Service NSW building*, she thought. Her curiosity piqued, and still smarting from her driving test failure, she walked in. Perhaps she'd learn something about how people used to drive that could help her the next time she took her driver's test.

There were several cars on display, and Adriana immediately fell in love with a black and white one.

"Wow, a 1957 Chevrolet," she read off the plaque to herself. The plaque also featured the history of this classic. As Adriana kept reading, she learned that this was one of the reasons why Earth's environment became polluted.

Adriana never noticed the older gentleman walking up to her. He stood for a few minutes, seemingly content to watch her admire the old car, and when she finished reading the plaque and turned around, she jumped in surprise to see him standing right behind her.

"Oh jeez, you snuck up on me."

"Sorry, Miss. My Name is Marcus Pinklewood. I own the museum. I usually do not get young people here. You like the 1957 Bel Air?"

"Is that its name? My dad named his 2119 International Hovercraft Wilson."

With a smile, Mr Pinklewood answered her question; "No, my dear, that was the model of the car. They did not give their cars pet names like we do now. For the most part, anyway."

"Aw, that's sad. I'd love to use one of these for my driver's license test. I bet I could drive it a lot better than those holographic simulators with their unrealistic challenges."

"My dear, this car is in perfect condition. It is driveable, fuelled up and ready to go. If you are interested, I could loan it to you for your test," said Mr Pinklewood.

"You're kidding. It really works?"

"Oh, I dabble in old stuff like cars, trains, and even old planes. I have an extensive collection. I would be more than happy to assist you in getting your driver's license. Would you like a go at it?"

"Sure, but is there a catch?"

"Just one: when you pass your test, tell your friends about the museum. We could always use younger patrons."

"You got yourself a deal."

"Excellent, my dear. I have a spare set of keys, so you may take the ones that are inside the car with you. I will drive it outside for you so you and your instructor can do your test, OK?"

"That'd be great, Mr Pinklewood. Thanks so much!"

"Don't mention it. Now get in there and break a leg."

"Break a leg?"

"Never mind, just go."

So, Adriana went back inside and once again walked up to the holographic receptionist. She had never felt more confident. Now she had a real, nuts-and-bolts car to use. No two-headed cats, no clown cars. Just her and the real road.

"Hello, I'm here for my driver's test," Adriana said with a positive grin.

"Sure thing! Here is your number on the queue. Just take a seat, and your instructor will be with you shortly...wait, were you not here before for a test?"

"Yes, but this time it will be different."

"Different? How is that?"

"I have my own vehicle outside. A 1957 Chevrolet Bel Air,"

The holographic receptionist looked at Adriana funny and said: "Excuse me, Miss, I need to check our procedures. I have never heard of this request."

The holographic receptionist disappeared and was gone for a minute or two. When the emoji returned, she gave Adriana her answer.

"It seems, Miss, that our records show it is still possible to take a driver's license test using an antiquated vehicle, and I can confirm that a 1957 Chevrolet Bel Air is indeed an antique and therefore qualifies you. Please wait for your instructor."

Adriana sat and waited, and five minutes later an elderly gentleman—a flesh and blood man, not an AI—in a blue jumpsuit came up to her. He clutched a clipboard under one arm and wore a hat which covered his face. She could, however, make out an impressive moustache.

"Ms Adriana McDougal? Are you ready for your test?"

"Yes, sir I am."

"Excellent. Let's go."

Adriana and the instructor stepped outside, and she saw the beautiful black and white 1957 Bel Air waiting for her. She got in and waited for her instructor to do the same.

"OK, Ms McDougal, let's start with something simple, like a lane change. When I give the signal, please merge into the right lane."

Adriana put the car in gear and started driving. She was surprised by the instructor's first instruction, for it was the same one instructor 4528 had given her. *I hope this isn't a bad omen*, thought Adriana as she kept her eyes on the road.

The Bel Air drove smoothly. The 'automatic transmission,' as the plaque had described it, made it so simple to use the vehicle. Avoiding the self-driven vehicles on the road was even easier; they avoided her. She chuckled.

"Is there something funny, Ms McDougal?"

"No sir. Just enjoying the drive, that's all."

"Now, please merge right," said the instructor.

Adriana nodded, ready to impress her human instructor. She sped up, merging smoothly into the right lane. So far, so good. *Again, just like last time,* she thought to herself.

Having completed that task, Adriana noticed the instructor making a note on his clipboard.

After a few minutes of driving, they came to a stop light. While at a stop light, a two-headed cat ran across the front of the car just as the light went green. She pounced on the brake and the two-headed-cat whipped around to stare at her and did a double meow as if saying 'thank you for not running over me,' before hurrying to the other side of the street.

So, they're still throwing these stupid tests at me, Adriana thought. This time, however, she was prepared.

The instructor made a quick note on his clipboard. He did not utter a single word.

After a few more kilometres of driving through neighbourhoods in Northport, practicing parallel parking and then reverse parking, the instructor gave her the last instruction: "You may now return to the Service NSW Centre, Ms McDougal."

Arriving at the centre, Adriana parked the Bel Air where she found it and turned off the ignition.

"I'm thrilled to say, Ms McDougal, that you have passed your driver's test. Your reactions to unexpected stimuli were excellent, and your driving was precise. Well done," the instructor said as he handed her a passing slip.

"Now, go get your driver's license."

Grabbing her slip and thanking the instructor, Adriana rushed out of the car, waited for him to exit, and locked the car doors. When she went back inside, she was practically sprinting.

After ten minutes, Adriana walked out into the sunlight with her new driver's license. She looked for the car, but it was not where she parked it. *Mr Pinklewood must have moved it*, she thought as she headed over to the museum. However, when she arrived, she was greeted by the strangest sight—or rather, a lack of sight. Where she museum had been before, there was now an abandoned, run-down building.

"What's going on?" She thought out loud. "It's not here!"

An elderly couple walking by overheard her confusion and stopped to ask if she was okay.

"I'm...I'm not sure. Wasn't there an antique car museum here before?"

The couple exchanged a sad look before the woman answered, "Yes dear. There was once an antique car museum here back in 2078, but it closed. People just lost interest in those old contraptions."

"But I was just inside an hour or so ago. I got to drive a 1957 Chevrolet Bel Air! I even took my driver's license with it. See, right here," she said as she showed them her new license.

"Well, good for you, dear, but you must have had a dream. This place has been closed since 2078. No one has leased it since then."

The older couple bid her goodbye and left Adriana standing there, looking into the empty carcass of the car museum.

"Did I have a dream?" she muttered. "No way. I visited the museum; I passed the test. I have my license. It had to be real."

Just then, someone tapped her shoulder. She turned and saw Mr Pinklewood standing there with a big smile on his face.

"Mr Pinklewood! What's going on?"

"Nothing, my dear. Everything is fine."

"But the museum, the cars. Nothing's there. How can that be?"

"It is a long story, so let me give you the short version. Back in the mid-2030s, the world started choking with all the pollution that came from the use of fossils fuels. This led to major changes, and the accelerated production of electric vehicles. Later, governments worldwide enacted a law that forbade the use of gas combustion vehicles. The production of said cars was brought to a complete halt, which led to increased production of more electric, hydrogen and then nuclear vehicles. Yet, a few individuals loved these old classics and formed a secret society known as 'The Ignition Illuminati,' which has existed in the shadows ever since."

"Let me guess: you're a member?"

"Yes Ms McDougal, I am. And now, so are you."

"Wait, so I'm a member of the Ignition Illuminati? How is that possible?" Adriana asked, the gears in her mind whirring. She still didn't understand how the building could suddenly disappear, or where the car had gone. She also realised that she had never told Mr Pinklewood her surname.

"And how do you know my name?" She demanded.

Mr Pinklewood just smiled and reached into his pocket. He pulled out a fake moustache, placed it over his lip and smiled at her.

She was gobsmacked.

"You were the instructor! Why?"

"Because you did a wonderful job driving one of the Ignition Illuminati's most prized possessions. You not only passed your driver's license test, but your initiation in the Ignition Illuminati. Now, if you don't mind, I'd like for us to go on a walk. There is a lot I need to pass on to you."

Mr Pinklewood took her arm and started telling Adriana the secrets of the Ignition Illuminati. As she tried to take in everything he said, she still struggled to believe that somehow, she had stumbled upon a world of antique auto enthusiasts who had been guarding the mystery and history of these classic vehicles with unwavering dedication and passion. As Mr Pinklewood continued to impart all the Ignition Illuminati's hidden knowledge, Adriana's disbelief faded. Instead, she was overcome by a sense of awe and privilege, knowing that she was now a part of this exclusive circle, entrusted with the preservation of humanity's automotive heritage for generations to come.

The Best Christmas Present

Christmas has always been a joyous occasion for our family. The environment and ambiance are always conducive to joy, with the twinkling lights on the tree and the warmth of togetherness. It is, without a doubt, our favourite time of the year. But this year, there is a palpable emptiness that hangs in the air, casting a shadow over our festive preparations. Ruby, our beloved Labrador, passed away at the start of the year, leaving a void in our hearts that has proven impossible to fill.

As our family gathers around the dining table, the melancholy of Ruby's absence weighs heavily. She had been a part of our lives and, of course, our Christmas celebrations for as long as our children can remember. Her tail wagging, her excited barks, and her eyes gleaming with anticipation of table scraps always added an extra layer of joy to the holiday season.

With a sigh, Sarah, our youngest, starts carving the roast turkey. Tears well up in her eyes as she looks to the floor beside her chair, likely remembering how Ruby used to sit by her side, patiently waiting for a morsel to fall. The rest of the family tries to muster up smiles, but the sadness is too profound. Rather than bring us together, this holiday season serves only to remind us of how we've lost a beloved member of our family. We still have each other, but in some way none of us can describe, we feel alone.

Just as we are about to begin the Christmas meal, we hear a familiar sound: a scratch at the front door followed by a muffled bark. We exchange puzzled glances around the table. It cannot be Ruby. She has been gone for a year, and there is no way she is standing outside the door. "Must be a stray," chimes in Pauly, our oldest.

But the scratching persists, louder this time, accompanied by a more urgent bark. As the family patriarch I get up from the table, a mixture of hope and confusion swirling in my mind. I approach the front door cautiously, not sure why. I know it will be a stray. It has to be. There is no other reasonable explanation.

When I open the door, the look on my face must be that of pure astonishment. My eyes go wide, my jaw drops. I stand there, utterly stupefied. There, standing on the doormat, is a Labrador. Her tail wags furiously, eyes sparkling with recognition. She is not Ruby; I am sure of it. But she looks exactly like her.

I kneel to embrace the dog. "Ruby, is it really you?" I whisper, my voice trembling with disbelief. The rest of the family rushes to the door, and when they see the dog, they are overcome by joy and wonder.

She bounds inside, her joyous barks filling the house once more. We turn to each other for confirmation of what we are seeing, unable to believe our eyes. She is not Ruby, and she is Ruby. She recognises all of us.

As the family surrounds the dog, showering her with hugs and tears of happiness, we noticed a collar around her neck. On it is a tag with a message: *Merry Christmas! I am home! My name is Betsy!*

We spend the rest of the evening with Betsy, telling her all about our year and how much we miss Ruby. She just wags her tail and barks at the conversation, as if she understands us. Our conversation becomes boisterous as our spirits rise. Our Christmases are always wonderful, but this one takes the cake. Still, I cannot help but wonder to whom Betsy belongs. She is clearly someone else's dog, but her tag leaves no clue as to whose. The best thing to do, I think, is wait until the owner comes around or starts putting up missing posters.

We finish our meal—Betsy of course gets a bunch of scraps—and we are all gathered in the lounge for coffee and dessert when the doorbell rings.

My wife Mary goes and answers the door and finds a couple with a little girl who is holding a leaflet in her hand. Her eyes are red and puffy, as if she has been crying.

"Have you seen our dog, Betsy?" she asks.

Mary ushers them into the lounge, whereupon, seeing Betsy, the little girl throws all the leaflets on the floor and rushes to give her dog a big hug.

The Pattersons explain that they had just moved into Newport a few weeks ago when their dog Betsy disappeared, and they were fearing the worst. Without Betsy, their little girl Andrea was inconsolable, so they decided they would go door to door on Christmas Day and hope for the best. They hardly expected to find her in someone else's house!

We ask the Pattersons if they had lunch. They had not, so Mary goes to the kitchen to warm up the leftovers and I take them to the dining room, along with Betsy and the rest of our clan.

As the Patterson eat their Christmas meal, we chat and Betsy gets more scraps, much to her delight.

"You're gonna get so fat!" Andrea squeals, even as she holds out more leftovers for Betsy to scarf up. She polishes them off and licks the little girl's hand, and she gives her dog a big hug. My children come over to pet her, and they all laugh as she leans up to lick each of their faces.

"Do you have a dog? There's an old dog door out front, but I don't see any pets," Mr Patterson asks.

"We had a Labrador named Ruby. She looked exactly like Betsy, actually. But she passed away early in the year," I answer.

"Oh, I'm so sorry," Mrs Patterson says sympathetically. I give her a thankful nod.

"We were all pretty surprised when Betsy showed up at our doorstep. I think some part of us thought that Ruby had come back somehow. Grief does crazy things to people, you know?" Mrs Patterson smiled.

"We completely understand. Andrea thought every Labrador she saw on the street was Betsy coming back home. She'd run up to them shouting 'Betsy!' and scare them off! I felt so bad for their owners," she says. We all chuckle at that and talk for a little while longer about our pets before I ask another question.

"How did Betsy get the dog tag with that inscription?"

Mr Patterson looks puzzled and gets up to inspect the dog tag. When he turns back to me, he just shrugs.

"That's not our tag," he says. "I wonder who put it there."

We fall silent at his words, but we all know that love has a way of returning when it is most needed. This Christmas, we've gotten two presents: new friends and a miracle in Betsy. In a way, Ruby has returned to us.

Share Market

In the heart of the dense, untouched wilderness, where the ancient, towering trees whispered secrets of centuries long past, a group of hunters embarked on an extraordinary adventure. These were not your ordinary hunters, however. They had no language to speak off, but through their grunts, they knew each other as what might be translated to 'The Primitives.' These hunters were dedicated to preserving their hunting rituals, as bizarre and unique as they were. Their communication comprised grunts, which were sometimes misunderstood.

On a crisp, dew-laden morning, five members of this enigmatic group gathered at the edge of the forest. Each of them was dressed in primitive hunting attire; their bodies were draped in rough-hewn animal pelts and their feet were wrapped in moccasins. Over their shoulders hung bows and quivers of arrows, and they had flint knives at their hips, the tools of their ancestors.

The leader of the group stood tall, his long hair flowing wildly in the wind. He was the torchbearer, a role handed down through generations. The Primitives believed in living in both worlds, spiritual and primitive, and today was a celebration of that duality.

As the sun pierced through the towering canopy, they ventured deeper into the forest, their senses attuned to every rustling leaf and chirping bird. The group was bound by their shared need for survival. Each step they took was deliberate and measured, respecting the age-old ways of their indigenous ancestors.

The forest was alive with secrets as they quietly moved through the underbrush, their eyes scanning for signs of their quarry. Using his expertise as a tracker, the leader could identify faint indications of animal movement, leading the group to their target. Their hearts beat with anticipation as they neared a herd of deer, feeling the thrill of the hunt.

They put their primitive weapons to use, and with utmost precision, they took down their targets. As they moved in to inspect the spoils of their hunt, a sense of reverence overcame them. It wasn't just about the kill; it was about the connection to their ancestral past, the respect for the creatures they harvested and the bond they shared with nature.

After the successful hunt, The Primitives gathered around a fire they had started with flint and tinder. They roasted the deer meat on a spit and feasted in silence, savouring the fruits of their labour and the ancient flavours that permeated the forest. The flickering flames cast dancing shadows on their faces, and for a moment, they were transported back to the time of their ancestors, in a long-forgotten past.

As the day waned and the shadows grew long, The Primitives extinguished the fire and walked to the end of the forest where their duffel bags were waiting for them.

Slowly they disrobed, their hearts heavy with nostalgia as they shed their primitive attire. Underneath, they revealed Bonds underwear and t-shirts.

It was time to return to the contemporary world, leaving behind the primeval connection they had forged with nature. With a sense of reverence and ceremony, they bid farewell to the forest that had been their home for a day. In a nearby clearing, concealed by the dense foliage, modern vehicles (a Mercedes, a Tesla, an Audi and two Lexus') awaited them.

"See you in the office," said Lester, the leader of the group. "Remember, we have the meeting on the ACME Ventilation Corporation and the Humongous Air-Con Company merger to discuss." His fellow venture capitalists nodded in the affirmative and responded with: "We'll see you in the office at 7." As they got into their automobiles and drove away from the wilderness in their sleek, air-conditioned SUVs, they left behind no trace of their passage, a testament to their dedication to both the past and the present.

The Primitives had undertaken their journey to the primitive not merely for the thrill of the hunt, but to reaffirm their place in the ever-evolving tapestry of history. As they sped away from the ancient forest, they took with them the memories of a day spent living as their ancestors did, and the knowledge that, in a world of constant change, there was value in connecting with the timeless traditions of the past, even if only for a fleeting moment: the hunt, the kill and the feast.

Besides, it helped them make a killing in the share market!

195

About the Author

The Cuban Revolution presented José with one of his many life challenges. José was born in La Habana, Cuba, and when the government was overthrown in 1959, he got on a plane alone and arrived at an orphanage in the small town of Washington, Georgia. He was only eleven years old. He did not get to see his parents again until he was eighteen years old and had graduated from high school in Atlanta, Georgia.

He studied Business Administration at Georgia State University. From university, he headed into the realm of finance, working for the First National Bank of Atlanta (now Wells Fargo) before transitioning into the world of financial consulting as a project manager, travelling to many assignments in the United States, Europe, and Australia.

Currently, José is working on a sequel to his novel *Books, Pens & Larceny*, which should be out in late 2024.

When José is not writing you can find him sitting at the local shopping centre mall, watching people, and getting inspirations for his future characters. If he is not there, he is reading or spending time with his wife taking long, leisurely walks around the Camden area.

***

Of course, your comments and reviews are always welcome. Please visit https://jfnodar.com.au/book-reviews/ and let me know what you thought of this anthology of short stories and poetry.

Good, bad, or indifferent, I welcome your honest opinion.

Thank you for your purchase!

José F. Nodar ©   2024

Other books by José F. Nodar

Books, Pens & Larceny

The Universe Between Us

Stories to Share with My Partner Book 1

Stories to Share with My Partner Book 2

Stories to Share with My Partner Book 3

Stories to Share with My Partner Book 4